NIGHTWORK

Other Dave Brandstetter Mysteries
by Joseph Hansen

Gravedigger
Skinflick
The Man Everybody Was Afraid Of
Troublemaker
Death Claims
Fadeout

Also by Joseph Hansen

Job's Year
Backtrack
A Smile in His Lifetime

A DAVE BRANDSTETTER MYSTERY

NIGHTWORK

Joseph Hansen

An Owl Book

HOLT, RINEHART AND WINSTON
New York

Published by Holt, Rinehart and Winston,
383 Madison Avenue, New York, New York 10017.

Published simultaneously in Canada by Holt,
Rinehart and Winston of Canada, Limited.

Library of Congress Cataloging in Publication Data
Hansen, Joseph, 1923–
Nightwork.
"An Owl book."
I. Title.
PS3558.A513N5   1984   813'.54   83-12846
ISBN 0-03-003679-8

First published in hardcover by Holt, Rinehart
and Winston in 1984.

First Owl Book Edition—1985

Designer: Marylou Redde
Printed in the United States of America
1 2 3 4 5 6 7 8 9 10

ISBN 0-03-003679-8

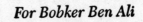

For Bobker Ben Ali

NIGHTWORK

1

The creekbed was paved with sloping slabs of concrete and walled by standing slabs of concrete to a height of ten feet. Weeds sprouted from the cracks between the slabs, showing that water seeped underneath, but the slabs were bone dry, bone white, and glared in the morning sun. Seeing them, no one not native here would credit that when the rains came, water would rush muddy, deep, and dangerous under this concrete-slab bridge.

Before the construction of these acres of shacky stucco houses in 1946, the creekbed was shallow, cluttered with boulders from the far-off mountains, shaded by live oaks, and clumpy with brush. He remembered it that way from the 1930s. Then, the only house out here was on a rise. He looked for it out the window of the Jaguar now. There it stood among trees, a white Victorian hulk with cupolas, scalloped shingles, long porches bristly with jigsaw work. The Gifford place. Back then, this flat land by the creek was all that remained of the once vast Gifford Ranch.

Los Angeles had expanded even before World War II. One by one, the upland sections of the ranch were sold off and turned into pleasant suburbs. During the Depression, only the well-off could buy land and build on it. But then the aircraft factories and shipyards put everyone to work. Goods became scarce. People saved. Housing couldn't be built during the war. Afterward, contractors couldn't put up houses fast enough. Buyers were waiting. Dave smiled wryly to himself. These places must have gone up in summer, while the creekbed was dry, and been sold in the dry autumn.

With winter came the rains. And the creek flooded, as it always had. And the bright new little houses were up to their windowsills in swirling water. Overnight, mattresses, sofas, armchairs that still smelled fresh from Sears and Montgomery Ward became bloated sponges. The new Philco radios crackled and expired. The new Fords, Chevies, Plymouths everyone had waited years to buy drowned behind the warped doors of garages in the dark. It was a headline scandal. It became a headline scandal winter after winter—until the County at last gouged out the creekbed and lined it with concrete slabs. Much too late.

He swung the Jaguar off the bridge and onto a street that paralleled the creek. The paving was patched and potholed. Cans, bottles, wrappers clogged the dusty gutters. Squat stucco shops lined the street. Many of the signs were old, sun-faded, crackled. A few were new—shallow tin boxes of fluorescent tubes, fronted by crisply lettered white plastic sheets. Stones or bottles had been thrown through some of these—LAUNDROMAT, DISCOUNT APPLIANCES, FRIENDLY LEO'S. Dave couldn't make out what Friendly Leo sold. The unwashed windows were empty.

The high white sign that said LIQUOR was intact. Under it, brown men in ragged clothes sat on the littered sidewalk with their backs against a storefront in whose windows pyramids of soft-drink cans, beer cans, wine bottles sparkled in the sun. The brims of straw hats were pulled low on the foreheads of the brown men to shield their eyes from the sun. They clutched rumpled brown sacks that appeared to hold beer cans or wine bottles. Some of them smoked. Now and then they spoke, but none of them smiled. They looked sad, aimless, and without strength.

Around a corner of the building, on a bumpy dirt parking lot where no cars waited—it was not yet eight in the morning—teenage boys tilted back their heads and poured soft drinks down their throats from bright cans, or jokily pushed each other, or halfheartedly wrestled, or leaned watching beside bicycles against the liquor store wall, which was spray-painted with graffiti. They were Chicanos. Some wore green jackets stenciled GIFFORD GARDENS on the back. Dave halted the Jaguar at a battered stop sign. The boys turned, nudged each other, stared at the car.

Dave drove on, disgusted with himself for bringing the car here. He glumly eyed the Blaupunkt radio in the burled wood of the dashboard. They might not strip a Jaguar here. Where would they fence the parts? But they would almost certainly steal a Blaupunkt. He could afford to replace it—that wasn't the point. He hated the notion of the car being broken into, violated. It would be like splintering an Amati. At another corner with a stop sign, he glanced into the side mirror. Boys in green jackets were following him on bicycles. He waited for a dirty white van marked in red with a plumber's name to turn out of the side street, then drove on. He pressed the accelerator pedal. The speedometer needle climbed. There was no engine roar—just quiet, powerful obedience.

But they continued to follow, patient as a pack of wolves. For maybe ten blocks. Then, suddenly, when he glanced at the mirror, they had vanished. On a corner lot fenced in sagging chainlink, a corrugated iron garage yawned blackly. Old Mustang automobiles clustered in front of it, waiting to be made new. And beside an old-fashioned red ice chest labeled Coca-Cola in scuffed white script, eight or ten black youths, some teenaged, some a little older, lounged, laughing with very white teeth. They sobered when they saw the Jaguar. They looked thoughtful, tilting their heads. They wore black jackets stenciled THE EDGE.

Dave drove on, frowning. Ought he to have brought Cecil Harris? Cecil was a young black who lived with Dave and shared his bed. And his dangers. Cecil was just out of the hospital where, for long, slow months, he had mended from bullet wounds. He was still weak and thin. He tired quickly. This day would be a scorcher. It would wring the boy out. He had begged to come along, but Dave had made him stay behind in the comparative cool of the rambling house in the tree-grown canyon. Dave doubted that Cecil's presence with him in the Jaguar would change attitudes in Gifford Gardens. He drove on, watching the mirrors for signs of The Edge.

He saw none until he reached Lemon Street. On this corner, flat-roofed, concrete-block buildings bracketed a courtyard with a big rubber tree. A sign read THE KIL-GORE SCHOOL. The school was fenced in brick, topped by neat, square-cornered iron bars. Small kids in tanktops and shorts, yellow, green, magenta, clutched books and lunches outside the gate. Anglos. Two or three orientals. No blacks, no browns. Through a glass door at the end of the courtyard, two striped gray cats looked out expectantly. He swung the Jaguar off the creekside street, and here were cramped, lookalike tract houses on narrow lots. Around the corner after him turned a 1973 Mustang that had been sanded down to its body steel and had black holes where its headlights used to be.

It parked across from the school, and he forgot about it until, five or six blocks onward, when he stopped at the curb in front of the Myers house, he glimpsed it in the door mirror as he left the Jaguar. The Mustang rolled to a halt a few doors back. He gave it only a glance, reached into the rear seat of the Jaguar for his jacket, put this on. No one got out of the Mustang. The windshield was dirty, but he thought two people were inside. He locked the Jaguar and went up a cracked sidewalk between patches of summer-seared grass where an old heavy wooden skateboard lay like a dead beetle on its back, one set of wheels missing. He climbed two short steps, pressed a door buzzer, and turned to look again at the Mustang. It sat there like a steel coffin.

The house door opened. A young man stood inside, naked except for briefs, hair uncombed, a stubble of dark beard. He winced at the brightness of the morning. His eyes were bleary and bloodshot. He licked cracked, dry lips, and croaked, "Who the hell are you, now?"

"Brandstetter." Dave had a card ready, and poked it at the closed aluminum screen door. "I'm from Pinnacle Insurance. Death-claims division. It's about Paul Myers. I need to see Angela Myers, please."

The young man grunted, snapped a catch on the screen door, pushed it open six inches, took the card and squinted at it. "Something wrong with the insurance?"

"Something wrong with how he died," Dave said. "Is Angela Myers here? Who are you?"

"Gene Molloy. I'm her brother." He turned and shouted into the house, "Angie? Some guy for you from the insurance company." He frowned at Dave through the silvery mesh. "It was an accident. He lost control of his rig. It went off a curve in Torcido Canyon and exploded and burned." He stepped back and shouted, "Angie!" This time, a female voice, high-pitched and short-tempered, shouted back.

Dave couldn't make out the words. Car doors slammed. Two black youths had gotten out of the Mustang, one muscular, the other fat, both in jackets marked THE EDGE. They came ambling up the sidewalk, looking at everything but the Jaguar. Molloy saw them. "What the fuck," he said.

"They followed me," Dave said. "They admire my car."

"Oh, shit." Molloy pushed the screen. "Get in here." He grabbed Dave's arm.

Dave held back. "I don't want them to dismantle it."

"Better it than you," Molloy said. "Get in here."

Dave got in. The room was dim, the air close, smelling of sweaty sleep and stale cigarette smoke. The sofa had been used as a bed. The rumpled sheet looked as if it covered a dead body. Empty beer cans stood on a cheap coffee table by the sofa. So did a fluted pink china ashtray full of butts. On a stack of magazines. *Scientific American?* At the foot of the sofa, on a wheeled tubular cart, a small television set showed blurred images without sound. Dave said, "Where's the telephone?"

"You don't need a telephone, you need a gun." Molloy snicked the lock on the screen door, shut the wooden door, locked it, fastened a chain that looked flimsy. "The cops will take all day getting here. They don't like messing with the gangs. You can get shot that way, knifed—you can get dead. Two of them died already this year."

"It seems a good neighborhood to leave." Dave pried open two of the thin slats on a blind and looked out. The Edge youths were walking slowly around the Jaguar, wagging their heads in admiration. But their hands were still in their pockets. "Why don't you move?"

"Paul and I bought this house." It was that angry female voice again. Dave let the blind go. It rattled loosely. "If we only rented, that would be different. But everybody knows what Gifford Gardens is. Who'd buy? Who'd be stupid enough to move here? We're stuck. I mean—I'm stuck." She turned in the door, calling into the back of the house. "If you two don't get a move on, you'll be late."

Children's voices called, each canceling out the message of the other. Didn't raising your young here amount to criminal child endangerment? They appeared. They looked all right, bright-eyed, rosy-cheeked, carrying books and lunch sacks.

Molloy told them, "Go out the back way. Cut across the vacant lot. Go down Lime Street."

"What's wrong?" Angela Myers stared.

"The Edge is out front," Molloy said. "Two of them. They followed Mister"—Dave's card was crumpled in his fist; he smoothed it and peered at it—"Mister Brandstetter here. He's got a big, fancy foreign car."

"Brian. Ruth Ann." Angela Myers gave her head a sharp tilt. The boy, fair hair in his eyes like a sheepdog's, Dave guessed to be about nine, the dark-haired girl perhaps eleven. They turned and disappeared. A door banged. Small shoes ran away quickly in the morning stillness. The Myers woman said to Molloy, "At least it's not the G-G's."

Dave studied her. She wore a starchy sand-colored outfit with white trim. A starchy little cap was on her head. Her shoes were stubby, with thick crepe soles. Something was wrong with her face—with the shape of it. The light was bad. He tugged a frayed cord on the blinds, and slatted sunshine came in. Her face was swollen as if from a beating. She'd applied thick pancake makeup, so the colors of the bruises didn't show, but he thought they were under there. One eye was still partly closed.

"What happened to you?" he said.

"My husband was killed," she said. "He was just a young

man. He was doing nightwork, trying to earn extra money to help out my parents, and it killed him. A man can't drive all day and all night too. You have to have sleep. I kept telling him. So what happened? He fell asleep at the wheel and drove off the road, and now he's dead. And how is that going to help anybody?"

"Did you bring the check?" Molloy asked Dave.

Glass shattered outside. Dave turned to the window. Through the slats, he saw the fat boy with the skateboard in his hand. He stepped back and watched while the muscular boy reached in through the broken window and opened the door of the Jaguar. "Damn!" Dave said, and lunged for the house door. He twisted the bolt and yanked. The door stopped with a jerk on the end of its short chain.

"Don't go out there." Molloy grabbed him from behind, pinning his arms.

"Listen!" Angela Myers ran to the window.

A siren wailed. Not far off. Dave shook free of Molloy. He pushed the door to, twitched the chain out of its slot, pulled the door wide, was stopped by the screen, scrabbled at its little lock. The Edge youths ran back to the Mustang. The fat one still had the skateboard in his hand. Did the muscular one have the radio? He couldn't. There hadn't been time. They fell inside the Mustang and slammed the doors. Dave stepped outside. The Mustang's engine thrashed to life, its tires screamed. Behind its blind eye sockets, it sped off up the street, swerving wildly. Dave ran down the walk. A Sheriff's car came up the street, gold and white, an amber light flashing on its roof. It rocked to a halt beside the Jaguar.

"They went that way," Dave said.

2

The Sheriff's car did not go that way. A brown man and a black man in suntans and sunglasses stepped out of it. They were young. The black one looked overfed. He eyed the Jaguar and turned his opaque gaze on Dave. He shook his head and smiled sadly. "This yours?" And when Dave nodded, "Not your smartest move. Beverly Hills where this belong." With a careful finger he touched a splinter of glass sticking up in the window frame. "They get anything?"

Dave bent and looked through the hole. The Blaupunkt was still in the dash. "I don't think so. I think they wanted the radio."

The Latino deputy scratched his chest and looked off up the bleak street where now nothing moved. "You take what you can get. You know what the unemployment figures are for teenage blacks around here? Sixty percent. Did you get a look at them? If we catch them, would you be willing to testify in court?"

From her front door, Angela Myers said, "No, he wouldn't. You know how they make life hell for you." She came at a soft-soled run down the walk. "They telephoned all night. They broke our windows, killed our dog, scared the kids so they couldn't go out and play."

9

The black deputy said, "He don't live around here."

"They'll find him," Angela Myers said. "You know that." She looked at Dave. "Paul, my husband—he testified against Silencio Ruiz. For a supermarket holdup. Other people saw it, but Paul was the only one brave enough to testify."

"Dumb enough." This was Molloy. He had put on faded blue jeans. A cigarette burned at the corner of his mouth and jumped when he spoke. "What did he think was going to happen? The Gifford Gardens gang would give him a medal?"

"He did the right thing," the black deputy said.

"What made you come here?" Dave said.

"Mr. Gifford called us." The Latino pointed. The Gifford mansion shone white in the sun behind its big trees. The windows glittered in the sun. "De Witt Gifford. He lives up there."

The black deputy chuckled. "Ain't much gets past old De Witt. Mind everybody's business. Like he was the King in his High Castle. Watches out that tower with binoculars. Nothing else to do."

Dave looked at the cupola. Maybe he imagined it, but he thought he saw a wink of reflected sunlight sharper than that off the curved window glass. The lenses of Gifford's Bausch & Lombs?

"Told the dispatcher some boys was after your car."

Dave said, "I'll have to go up and thank him."

"You'll have a hard time." The Latino deputy walked around the Sheriff's car to the driver's side. "He's got more chains and locks and burglar alarms than you can count. Guard dogs too. Nobody gets in there." Across the roof of the car where the amber light still winked, he said, "Those boys will be back at the Mustang garage, probably. You

10

want to drive with us, point them out to us?"

"Don't do it," Angela Myers said.

"Don't worry," the black deputy said. "I ain't going in there. No way."

"I'll call for backup." His partner dropped into the Sheriff's car and reached for the dashboard microphone.

"We'll need the marines," the black deputy said.

"It only adds up to a broken window," Dave said. "It's not worth risking life and limb for. I'll let it pass. I have work to do in this town."

"Get yourself another car," the black deputy said. "Look like you could buy a fleet for what this one cost." He stroked the lustrous dark brown finish. "You want one, if they remove certain parts it don't much matter." He grunted when he dropped onto the seat of the Sheriff's car. He closed the door. "I'm serious."

"I take every man who wears a large gun seriously," Dave said. "Thanks for coming. Thanks for your advice."

"Mrs. Myers?" This was the Latino deputy. He bent his head and peered past his partner. "Silencio. Ruiz. He hasn't been bothering you, has he?"

"What do you mean? He's in San Quentin."

"I mean your face. It looks like somebody beat you up. It wasn't him, was it?"

"I had a fall." She touched her swollen eye. "At the restaurant where I work."

"He's out on parole," the deputy said. "A week already. That's why I asked. Your husband—has Ruiz been bothering him?"

"My husband is dead," she said.

"I'm sorry to hear that. If Silencio bothers you, that will constitute breaking the provisions of his parole. Don't let him intimidate you. Call us right away, okay?" He smiled briefly, raised a hand, and the Sheriff's car rolled off down the empty morning street. The amber light was not winking anymore.

"I have to get to work." Angela Myers hurried toward the house. "I can't afford any more days off."

Gene Molloy started across the brown grass toward two narrow strips of cracked cement that were a driveway. "I'll drop you off."

"So you'll have the car to run around to bars all day, wasting gas?" She jerked open the screen door. "Like hell you will." Dave was right behind her. She marched for the rear of the house, and so did he. In a kitchen that smelled of burned toast, and where spoons leaned in cereal bowls on a steel-legged table with a yellow Formica top, she snatched up a soft leather handbag from a yellow Formica counter beside a steel sink, and reached for the back door.

"Please wait," Dave said. She swung around sharply, surprised and annoyed that he was still here. He said, "I have bad news. Call your brother and sit down, all right?" He turned a steel-legged chair with yellow plastic padded back and cushion out from the table. Crumbs strewed the seat. He brushed them off. She didn't move. She glared at him. He said, "Your husband didn't fall asleep. What happened to him was not an accident. Any more than what happened to your face was an accident."

She said, "Look, mister, I don't know who you think—"

Molloy appeared at the back screen door. "What's going on?" He came inside, glanced at angry Angela, scowled at Dave. "Listen, friend, this is my sister."

"Sit down, please." Dave hooked another chair by the leg with his shoe and swung it out from the table. "The Sheriff's lab men have been examining the wreckage of Paul Myers's truck. It's taken a week, but now they're sure. He

12

didn't have an accident. Someone attached an explosive device under the cab, and blew it up."

"No." Angela clutched Molloy's arm, as if her legs wouldn't hold her. She was more than surprised. She was frightened. She looked up into Molloy's unshaven sulky boy face, as if he could change the truth. "They wouldn't do that. Why would they? He was tired. He drove off the road."

Molloy regarded Dave. "You sure about this?"

"The technicians are sure. It was detonated by remote control. Someone followed him and set it off when he reached that particular curve. They meant for it to look like an accident. Trucks have gone off there before."

"Silencio," Molloy said. He helped Angela to a chair She collapsed onto it. She was shivering. Molloy said, "I'm calling the cops." He moved to leave the kitchen.

"Save your dime," Dave told him. "They're on their way. Lieutenant Jaime Salazar, Sheriff's homicide." He checked his watch. "He was supposed to meet me here. Is there any whiskey?"

"Huh?" Molloy gaped. Dave nodded at Angela. Molloy looked at her and understood. "Yeah, sure." He climbed on a chair and from a high cupboard brought down a fifth bottle with a red label, SLIM PRICE. He unscrewed the cap and poured from the bottle into a glass that had held orange juice. He pushed the glass at Angela. "Here. This will make you feel better."

"I can't go to work with liquor on my breath."

"You can't go to work anyway. You have to tell them about Ruiz in the courtroom, what he yelled when the judge sentenced him. He was going to kill Paul. Isn't that what you told Mom? He was going to kill Paul when he got out?"

She leaned back in the chair, sighed, shut her eyes. "They get excited and say crazy things. Mexicans."

13

"Angie, it had to be him. It happened just after he got out. You heard that deputy." He took her hand, folded the fingers around the glass. "Drink that, will you? You look like you're going to pass out." She opened her eyes, drank, made a face, shuddered. Molloy said to Dave, "Who in hell else could it be? Didn't it have to be him?"

"It was a sophisticated device," Dave said. "I understood Ruiz was a street punk."

"There's training shops in prisons," Molloy said.

Dave sat down. Angela sat with her eyes closed, the whiskey forgotten in her hand. He reached out and gently touched her arm. She opened her eyes.

"Mrs. Myers—who beat you up?"

A corner of her mouth twisted. "Who always beats women up? Husbands. You look old enough to know that."

Dave looked up at Molloy. Molloy seemed surprised. Dave said, "Didn't you do anything about it?"

"Me? I wasn't here. You think he'd let me live here? Forget it. Not for years."

"He wouldn't let you live off him," Angela said dully.

Molloy told Dave, "I came after he got killed. Has to be a man in the house. In Gifford Gardens? You better believe it. Anyway, Angie always wanted me here. It was Paul that hated my guts."

Angela found Molloy's hand and smiled up at him with gentle reproach. "He didn't. He just wanted you to stand on your own feet. As long as you could live here with us, free meals, free rent, pocket money, you never would. He did it for your own good. Just like Daddy and Mama."

"Oh, boy." Molloy gave a sour laugh and asked Dave, "Can you figure that? Just out of high school. Your folks kick you out, your brother-in-law kicks you out. No job, no money, no place to sleep. And they call it love."

14

"They call a lot of things love," Dave said, "and some of the most unlikely ones turn out to be just that."

Molloy snorted. Cigarettes lay on the table. He pulled out a third chair, sat on it, shook a cigarette from the pack, lit it with paper matches whose print urged him to complete his high-school education at home. He blew out the flame with a stream of smoke and asked Dave, "Does it make some difference to the insurance company if he was murdered or died by accident?"

"It could. In either case, I'd be here."

"What for?" Angela said. "I already told the police all I know. I don't know anything. Gene's right. It has to be Silencio, doesn't it? Ruiz?"

"Sometimes," Dave said, "we know things without knowing we know them. Paul Myers went for years without life insurance. Then, suddenly, a month ago, he took out a policy for a hundred thousand dollars." Dave glanced at the shabby kitchen, faded yellow paint, scuffed vinyl tile, crooked cupboard doors. "That's expensive. What happened to make him do that?"

She shrugged. "Ossie Bishop died. It scared Paul. It happened so fast. No warning. He didn't want to leave me and the kids and my folks high and dry."

"Ossie Bishop!" Molloy jumped up, making the movement noisy, scraping the chair legs. He went to the stove. A glass coffeepot stood there, half full, over a low flame. He turned up the flame. Anger was in the sharp twist of his wrist. "He'd have that jig in the house. He wouldn't have me—his wife's own brother."

"Ossie was Paul's best friend," Angela told Dave. "I didn't like having one of them in the house, but he wouldn't hear a word against Ossie. And that wife of his, Louella—big, fat, black thing. Always trying to be friendly, asking me to go to that nigger church with her, wanting our kids to play together. Paul didn't see anything wrong with it, but I don't believe in it. I wasn't raised that way."

"This is a mixed town," Dave said. "Surely, in school—"

"I don't let them go to public school. White kids get mugged and knifed and raped at public school in Gifford Gardens. That's the reason I waitress. So I can pay to send them to the Kilgore School."

"Was Ossie Bishop an independent trucker too?"

She nodded. "It was him who told Paul about the nightwork. He was doing it trying to save up enough to buy a second truck so his oldest boy could drive it when he got out of high school."

Molloy banged mugs onto the table among the milky cereal bowls, whose spoons tinkled from the jar. "Jesus, have you told Dad that? That even a nigger thinks of his own flesh and blood first? I'm sure as hell going to tell the old bastard."

"Gene," she said wearily, "that's all past and gone. It's no good eating yourself up inside over something that can't be changed. He's sick, anyway. Leave him alone. You never wanted to be a truck driver."

"I sure as hell never wanted to be a carpenter." Molloy brought the coffee pot and filled the mugs. "Not for free, for Christ sake. He paid his other apprentices. I was his kid— so I didn't get paid. Beautiful." He set the coffeepot back on the stove.

Dave asked Angela, "What happened to Bishop? A road accident?"

"He got sick. He was away from work a couple of days. Then he died. In the middle of the night. He couldn't get his breath. Louella called a doctor, but it was too late. Big healthy man, still young. It scared Paul."

16

Dave tasted the coffee. Hot but weak. He lit a cigarette. "When was Silencio Ruiz locked up?"

Angela wrinkled her forehead. "Two years ago? Eighteen months?" Her laugh was bitter. "The sentence was five years. It didn't mean anything, did it?"

"Not much," Dave said. "Ossie Bishop died a month ago?" He reached across the table for the ashtray. "I don't think Silencio Ruiz killed your husband."

3

A bove his raised coffee mug, Molloy squinted at him. "What the hell do you mean? What's Ossie got to do with it?"

"Ossie just got sick," Angela said.

"Maybe somebody made him sick," Dave said.

"What for?" Molloy twisted out his cigarette. "Paul fingered Silencio for that holdup. That's why Silencio killed him. Where does Ossie come in?"

"He got Paul the nightwork." Dave turned to Angela. "What was he doing up in Torcido Canyon at three in the morning? What was he hauling? Who was he working for?"

"He—never told me." The bag fell from her lap with a muffled thud. She snatched it up, rummaged in it, brought out a little mirror. She touched her bruises. "I'm a mess."

"You weren't curious about what he was doing? You said it worried you, how tired he was making himself."

"It paid well. That's all he said. He wanted to help my folks." She glanced at Molloy. "Our folks. Dad had a stroke. He was always strong as a horse, so naturally he didn't have any health insurance. They used up all their savings practically overnight—doctors, hospital bills. He's a carpenter, and you know how much work they've been getting lately. They were running out of money even before he got sick."

'What about the union?" Dave said.

Molloy's laugh was dry. "He didn't believe in unions. He wasn't going to shell out dues every month so some fat wop racketeer could sit with his feet up on a desk drinking beer while he earned a living for the son of a bitch."

Dave watched Angela apply fresh lipstick. Her hand trembled. He said, "Every man doesn't feel so responsible for his in-laws."

Molloy made a sound of disgust. "Dad bought Paul his first semi, started him out as an independent. Do you think he did the same for me when I got old enough? Forget it."

"Paul still owed him for the truck?" Dave asked.

"He paid that off long ago." Angela closed the lipstick and dropped it into the bag. "No. Dad was good to him when he needed help. Paul wouldn't forget a thing like that. Dad was in trouble. Paul did all he could."

"He doesn't sound like a wife-beater," Dave said.

"He was tired and strung out. He was taking pills to keep him awake. Amphetamines. Truckers always have them. Pass them around to their buddies at rest stops." The mirror was propped against her coffee mug. She dropped the mirror into the bag now and zipped the bag closed. "He wasn't mean. It was too much pressure for him. He was frantic, and I got him sore, nagging at him to give it up. He was kind and patient before." Her eyes leaked tears. She wiped them away with a finger. "You ask the kids."

"Amphetamines can make a man edgy," Dave said.

"Where the hell is your County friend?" Molloy was reading a five-dollar digital watch. "Silencio will be in Mexico by now. In Argentina." He laid his cigarette in the ashtray, picked up his mug. "What did you say this deputy's name is?"

"Salazar," Dave said.

"Jesus, another spic." Molloy choked on coffee. "Don't

they hire white people anymore? What's a guy named Salazar going to do about a guy named Ruiz?"

"Whatever has to be done," Dave said.

Angela got to her feet, clutching her bag. "I have to get to work."

"You'd better phone in sick," Dave said.

"I've already been off a week. They'll replace me with some other girl. I have to have that job." She unzipped the bag again to dig keys out of it. "I have children to feed and bills to pay."

"I don't like to sound heartless or anything," Molloy said, "but you've got a big fat insurance check coming."

"Hah." She looked glumly at Dave. "Have I?"

Dave gave her a little half smile. "Possibly. Tell me Louella Bishop's address."

"She left town. I don't know." Angela pushed open the back screen door. "I don't care. I'm glad she's gone."

"Lieutenant Salazar will want to talk to you."

"Paul's dead," she said, "and you say someone killed him. That's all I know. There's nothing to talk about." The screen door fell shut behind her. He went to it. The backyard was patchy grass, clotheslines, a twiggy lemon tree. She hoisted a garage door that creaked. "Tell him I couldn't wait." She went into the garage, a car door slammed, an engine started, stalled, started again. The motor raced hard and loud for a moment. Smoke poured out the garage door.

Dave asked Molloy, "What restaurant is it?"

"Cappuccino's," Molloy said. "They won't like the cops coming to talk to her there." He made to pass Dave, to go out and stop her. But the car, a dented, ten-year-old Toyota station wagon in need of a wash, bucked backward out of the garage and rolled quickly from sight along the side of the house. It jounced noisily across the gutter out in front. Molloy ran barefoot through the house. The front screen

20

door rattled. Molloy called, "Angie, wait!" But the car went off up the street. Dave heard it.

He began opening drawers in the kitchen. Papers lay in one of the drawers. Supermarket tally tapes, receipts for electricity, water, gas, phone. Canceled checks in bank envelopes, old income-tax forms, property-tax forms, ownership registrations for a 1973 Toyota and an eighteen-wheel rig, and loan papers on the house at 12589 Lemon Street. He pocketed a check and a bankbook. There were no slips of paper with addresses scribbled on them.

Molloy came in. "What the hell are you doing?"

"Looking for Louella Bishop's address. Your sister is too frightened to tell me about Paul's nightwork. Maybe Louella Bishop will tell me."

"Frightened? Come on." Molloy opened a refrigerator door taped with children's watercolor drawings. He brought out a can of beer. The drawings fluttered when he closed the refrigerator door. "You don't ask your old man questions when he keeps putting a fist in your mouth. She doesn't know. Why would she lie to you?"

"You don't think Paul beat her up," Dave said. "It surprised the hell out of you when she said that. You didn't like him, but you know he wasn't a wife-beater."

Molloy pried up the tab opener on the beer can. "Then it had to be Silencio, didn't it?"

Dave shook his head. "She didn't know until this morning that he was out of prison. Anyway, what would be the point?"

Molloy sat at the table and took a long swallow from the beer can. He wiped his mouth with the back of his hand and belched. "He probably came looking for Paul, and when Paul wasn't here, Ruiz beat up Angie just for openers, and she's scared to say so because he's still running around loose." He looked at his watch again. "And the way this friend of yours is moving on the case, he always will be. 'Scuse me. You want a beer?" He half offered to get up.

"It's a little early for me." Dave judged Molloy to be twenty-five. He was already thick through the middle. It wouldn't take many more years of drinking beer all day to turn him to flab. "Where's the telephone?"

Molloy told him. The instrument sat on a spiral-bound leatherette book with lettered leatherette tabs on the page edges. He laid the book open at *B*, but the address for Ossie Bishop was local. He flipped pages ahead, pages following. Nothing. He lifted the phone, slid the book back under it.

He opened a door and saw bunk beds, stuffed animals, toy trucks, a poster of the Dukes of Hazzard. He closed the door, took a few steps, opened another. The bed was unmade. Women's clothes lay around: skirts, blouses, jeans, crushed panty hose. Makeup and crumpled tissues littered a dressing table. He rolled open closet doors. A lone blue polyester suit hung on a wooden hanger. It smelled of drycleaning. Did she mean to bury him in that? There were two tan windbreaker jackets, a corduroy jacket, brown dress slacks, some heavy plaid wool shirts.

"You have to have permission," Molloy said.

Dave didn't answer, didn't turn. He went through the pockets of Myers's clothes and found a small address book. Knuckles rattled the front screen door. The door buzzer sounded. Molloy said, "For Christ sake, now what?" and went away. No new out-of-town address for Bishop was in the small book, but Dave pocketed it anyway and shut the closet. Where had Myers kept business records? Dresser drawers? Nothing but clothes. Drawers were under the closet doors, and he crouched and opened one. Sheets, towels, blankets. He shut that drawer and opened the other. Papers lay there, flimsies, dim carbon copies, pink, blue, green. He grabbed a handful, stuffed them into an inside jacket pocket, closed the drawer with a foot, and went to find Molloy.

Jaime Salazar was saying, "Then there's no need to bother your sister at work. You can tell her." He was slim and dapper in a lightweight blue denim suit, maroon shirt and socks, blue knit tie. Heat had already begun to gather in the small living room, but Salazar looked cool. His skin was smooth, pale brown. He wore a neat mustache and sunglasses. "There you are," he said to Dave.

"What kept you?" Dave said.

"Trying to find an ex-convict called Silencio Ruiz. Paul Myers's testimony got him convicted of armed robbery year before last. He said he'd kill Myers when he got out. He's out two days and pow—Myers is killed."

Molloy grinned at Dave. "What did I tell you?"

"That bomb was no amateur effort," Dave said.

"He could have paid somebody to make it for him."

Dave said, "Why would he bother? Silencio was a street-gang member. Whatever happened to switchblade knives?"

"He's disappeared. He was supposed to see his parole officer yesterday. He only slept at his parents' house his first night. They haven't seen him since. His gang has a hangout at a liquor store down by the creek. They haven't seen him either—not since Myers's so-called accident was on the breakfast news."

"What reason would he have to run," Dave said, "if the whole world believed it was an accident?"

"When we catch him, we'll ask him." Salazar looked out through the open blind. "Did that happen to your car here, this morning?"

"Gifford Gardens doesn't have a red carpet," Dave said.

Molloy said, "Care for a beer, Lieutenant?"

"Orange Crush?" Salazar asked wistfully.

"I'll look. Maybe she keeps some for the kids." Molloy went away whistling, pleased with himself.

Salazar tilted his beautiful head at Dave. "You don't buy it? You think the wife did it for the insurance money?"

"She says he beat her. It wasn't smart to tell me that. It also wasn't true. She's scared of whoever beat her. Since he's dead, that makes no sense. I think whoever beat her also killed him. Why they would do that puzzles me. But if it was to keep her from telling what she knows, it had the desired effect."

"If it wasn't her, what's left for you to do?"

"Life insurance can be tricky," Dave said. "Ever hear of a two-year conditional clause? It lets the company back off if it turns out the insured lied to them. Paul Myers outlined for Pinnacle the kind of cargo he hauled—routine, machine parts, unfinished furniture, clothing. Nothing out of the way. Nothing anybody would want to blow him up for. So maybe he was lying."

"If he was—she won't get anything?"

"Something. Not a hundred thousand."

Molloy came in and held out a frosty purple can. Salazar took a step backward and put his hands behind him. He said in an appalled voice, "Grape?"

"It's all there is," Molloy said.

"No, thanks," Salazar said. "Thank you very much."

"I'd better go," Dave said, and went.

24

4

Guava Street had no sidewalks. Little enough remained of its paving—bleached, cracked islands of blacktop that stood inches above the dirt level of the street. The Jaguar rocked and rumbled. Weeds edged the street, seedy, sun-dried. There were a few fences, chainlink, picket, grapestake. The houses, on narrow lots, were smaller here, the stucco sometimes broken away, showing chicken wire and tarpaper. Under untrimmed, drooping pepper trees, the composition roofs were losing their green and silver coatings. Rooflines sagged.

Small black children, in paper diapers, rompers, jeans, or nothing at all, tottered and squatted, hopped and hollered in dusty yards of pecking chickens, sunflowers, hollyhocks. Auto bodies rusted in a few yards. A rope holding a tire swung from a tree branch. Scruffy dogs lay in patches of shade, tongues hanging. On stoops, on sunny roofs, cats washed themselves or dozed. Other than the children, he saw only occasional women, young and pregnant in cheap bright cotton prints and hair straighteners, or old and bony, or old and fat. No teenage boys.

Mount Olivet Full Gospel Church might have been a warehouse but for its location in a grove of walnut trees and its stucco steeple. It was built of cinder block. Through a fresh coat of pale yellow paint the ghosts of Spanish graffiti showed. The windows were narrow and sparse. There was no stained glass. Louvers, the pebbled panes amber-colored. A strip of clean concrete lay alongside the church and he followed it in the Jaguar. A typical Gifford Gardens house sat behind the church. He climbed the stoop and pushed a doorbell button. LUTHER PRENTICE, D.D., was on a weather-yellowed business card tacked beneath the bell push.

But it was a reedy, butter-colored woman in an apron who opened the door. Good cooking smells rushed out at Dave through the screen. The woman dried her hands on the apron. Her hair was abundant, soft, and white. She gave him a quizzical smile, blinking, tilting her head a little. "Yes. Good morning." Beyond him she saw the Jaguar and her soft brown gaze rested on it a moment. "How can I help you?" He told her who he was, and offered his card. Like Gene Molloy earlier, she took it gingerly through a narrow opening between screen and doorframe. She read it and said, "I'm afraid we have all the insurance we need."

"I'm not selling it," Dave said. "I'm a death-claims investigator. I'm looking into the death of Paul Myers."

She frowned a little. "Was he a member of this congregation? I don't remember the name."

"He was a friend of a member of this congregation." Beyond her, Dave glimpsed movement in a room dark by contrast to the blazing sunlight outdoors. "Ossie Bishop. I'm told he died recently too. I'd like to talk to his wife, Louella, but I hear she's moved."

A tall, lean old man, very black, bald, with a fringe of springy white hair, appeared beside the woman. He took off horn-rimmed spectacles and peered at Dave. "She and her children left right after the funeral—I'd say it was more

26

than just leaving. I'd call it running away."

"You men talk," the woman said. "I've got chickens and a whole lot of ribs to barbecue." She faded from sight. Her tall, straight old husband pushed open the screen door. He said, "Come in and sit down. Perhaps you'd enjoy to have a little iced tea." As Dave went indoors past him, the man peered, squinting, at the blazing morning. He too saw the Jaguar and was quiet for a moment. He closed the screen door and latched it. "I hope the damage to your car didn't happen here."

"It was my own fault." Dave waited among folding chairs in a room surprisingly large. Walls had been knocked out, hadn't they? This place had to do as parish house as well as rectory. The good cooking smells were strong here. A pair of long, fold-down tables rested against a side wall. He had glimpsed others set out in the walnut grove. There was going to be a picnic today or tonight. Luther Prentice, D.D., closed the wooden house door and said, "There is going to be a church picnic tonight at six." He smiled. "You're welcome to come." He motioned with a long hand whose nails were large and pink and whose palm was pale. "Please sit down. These are not comfortable chairs, but they are what we have, and we are thankful for them."

"I appreciate the invitation to the picnic." Dave sat. The chair was steel, with a thin seat cushion. The metal of the back made a cold band below his shoulder blades where jacket and shirt were sweaty. "But the Sheriff's men advise me not to drive that car here anymore. They cite the high unemployment rate in Gifford Gardens as responsible for the risk to property."

"It is a beautiful car." Prentice's smile was slight as he sat down. He wore dark suit trousers and a neat plaid cotton shirt, buttoned below a large larynx that made his voice deep. "Beauty is so often mankind's undoing. The Sheriff was right. It is too bad he couldn't have warned you before the damage was done."

"Perhaps then I wouldn't have taken him seriously. Reverend Prentice, do you know where Louella Bishop ran away to? It's vital that I talk to her."

"I'll get you the address," Prentice said. "But I don't know that talking to her will be of any use. She is a frightened woman. Her husband's death frightened her. Ah, I'm forgetting the iced tea." He got to his feet, went as stiffly as a man on stilts down the long room, and pushed open a swing door. Dave rose and opened the front door so he could watch the Jaguar. He couldn't be sure who, from inside what house, had seen him driving here. He saw no one now. Off to the west, the curved glass of the towers of the Gifford place sparked sunlight above their treetops. Dave heard Prentice returning. "I'm sorry," he said. "It appears to be lemonade today."

"That's fine." Dave smiled and took the icy glass.

"Here is Louella Bishop's address." Prentice had written it in an old-fashioned angular hand on a slip of paper. Dave glanced at it and pushed it into a pocket. Halcon. A small town in a valley of boulder-strewn hills inland from Escondido. Avocado country, he seemed to remember. Citrus too. Hard blue skies. Prentice said, "A family she used to work for. Please—sit down."

"Thank you." Dave sat. So did the tall old man. "Paul Myers died in a truck crash. His wife says he was a good friend of Ossie Bishop. It was when Bishop died so suddenly that Paul took out life insurance. Did you know Bishop well? You conducted the funeral, am I right?" Prentice nodded. Dave said, "What can you tell me about the reason for his death?"

"Very little. It was sudden—that was all. He was here in church with her on Sunday. By Friday he was dead. Before sunrise. I know he was working hard, because she said so. Working day and night. But he was a robust man. She said it was a heart attack brought on by overwork. It's possible, I suppose."

Frowning thoughtfully, he paused and sipped his lemonade. Dave tried his. Nothing frozen about it. It was what it was supposed to be, and it was not too sweet.

Prentice said, "Sometimes those that look the strongest are really frail. To survive in this world, a black man has to start working early in life, and sometimes they burn out early." He gave his glossy bald head a worried shake. "But she was afraid to talk about what took place that Thursday night. It wasn't like her. She was talkative as a rule, open and easy." He smiled to himself. "Always could find something to laugh about, didn't matter what. She was a great help here at the church, and she lifted all our spirits with her gift of laughter. We already miss her sorely. However, she was normally a slow-moving woman, and she moved as if the Devil himself was after her when it came to leaving Gifford Gardens once Ossie was in the ground. Funeral was Monday morning. She was on her way south with the children and her worldly goods by nightfall."

"That didn't give her much time to sell the house," Dave said. "Or did she only rent? What about his truck?"

"House wouldn't be a problem. People around here dying for a roof to get in under that they can afford." Prentice furrowed his brow. "As to the truck, most likely the boy drove it, the oldest, Melvil. His father hoped for him to be a driver too, once he finished high school. It would be a means of livelihood for the family, wouldn't it, now that the father is gone? The investment in one of those big trucks must be considerable."

"In the neighborhood of a hundred thousand dollars, these days," Dave said.

"Speaking of Melvil reminds me." Prentice lifted his glass to take a final swallow from it. "He said something to his mother at the graveside. That she called the wrong doctor. He seemed angry with her, though he spoke low."

"Who would have been the right doctor?"

"Most of us around here go to Dr. Hobart. He is a member of this congregation. Most Christian man I know."

"Did Melvil name the doctor his mother called?"

"He was something to do with the trucking business." Prentice took off his glasses and wiped them with a white, sharply creased handkerchief. "That's all Melvil said. And white. Melvil didn't like that." Prentice looked sorrowful, putting his spectacles on again, pushing away the handkerchief. "I regret it very much when youngsters feel that way, but so many do now. 'A new commandment I give unto you—that ye love one another.' That's what the Lord Jesus told us. That's what I preach, is love. But the young men don't come." He stared forlornly past Dave at the door Dave had left standing open. "Those come that don't need the sermon. But the young men don't come." He sighed. "It's why we're having this barbecue, you know. There won't be any preaching. There'll just be food. They are hungry, most of them." He shook his head. "They take it out in hatred. Enmity between the races—it's brought nothing but grief and sorrow and loss. But they are hating now more than ever. These gangs—black against brown. I don't know where it's going to end. We're located here, where we are sitting now, right in the middle of it. Next block"—he held up a long black thumb—"you won't hear anything but Spanish spoken. They come at night and paint their marks all over the walls. Obscenities too. But that's not the worst." He eyed Dave bleakly. "They are killing each other. Killing. And the innocent too. Children. They drive by and shoot, and it could be anybody gets hit. The

30

police, they try to stop it, but they get killed too. We are in the last days, it appears."

Dave set down his glass. "Who was the undertaker?"

"Wrightwood." Prentice got up when Dave did. "This Paul Myers—why are you investigating his death?"

Dave told him, and the minister's eyes widened. He said, "Then Louella Bishop was frightened. I was right."

"I don't know." Dave started for the sun-bright doorway. "Paul Myers was murdered, so perhaps it's natural that his widow should be frightened. But what frightened Louella Bishop? If her husband died of natural causes, why did she run so far, so fast?" He held out his hand. "Thank you for the address."

"Whatever I can do." Prentice shook Dave's hand. His face changed. He lunged past Dave and flung open the screen door. "Get away from there!" He went down the steps. "You hear me? Drop those things!"

Two black kids raced off down the driveway, hubcaps flashing in their hands. Prentice ran after them at an old man's run. Dave passed him. The car the boys piled into was another Mustang, its rear end smashed in. The bent trunk lid flapped high as the car careened away up Guava Street, a door still hanging open, legs kicking from the open door, laughter shouting from the open door. Dave halted on the grass in front of the church. Prentice came panting up to him.

Dave said, "Where did they get that name—The Edge?"

Prentice wiped his face with the neat handkerchief. "From a song—'Don't push me, 'cause I'm close to the edge, trying not to lose my head.'" He gazed dismally off up the street. He told Dave, "I am so terribly sorry."

"It's not your fault," Dave said.

5

The high wall around the grounds of the Gifford place was almost invisible under matted honeysuckle vine. So were the pillars that held the tall iron gates. It took time to locate an intercom outlet among the leafage. The outlet looked new. It probably had to be replaced fairly often. He pressed a rectangular white plastic button. From here, because the trees were large and shaggy, he couldn't see the cupola where he supposed De Witt Gifford sat. Beyond the gates, the grounds were neglected. Oleanders tall as trees crowded the drive, dropping the last of their blossoms, pink, white. Roses bloomed blowsy on long canes in flowerbeds rank with wild oats and milkweed. Dark ivy covered the ground and climbed the tree trunks. The intercom speaker crackled.

"I'm busy." The voice was an old man's, brittle. "Who are you? What do you want?" Dave told him. The snappishness went out of the voice. "Oh, yes, of course. How very— gentlemanly of you to come. Please wait."

The wait was a long one. Dave spent it in the car. That seemed the best way to guard the car. The sun beat down. He lit a cigarette, but it tasted dry, and he put it out. He wished for a fresh glass of Mrs. Prentice's lemonade. Below him lay the roofs of Gifford Gardens, drab gray, drab green, drab red, under a drab brown sky. He located the big rubber tree that marked the Kilgore School, the walnut grove where the church steeple rose, the pepper trees on Guava Street. Elsewhere in Gifford Gardens, trees were scarce. The developers in 1946 had bulldozed the oaks. Now dogs began to bark—big dogs, by the sound of them. Dave got out of the car.

Down the drive beyond the gates came a motorized invalid's chair. The wire spokes of its wheels glittered in the darts of sunlight through the oleanders. In the wheelchair rode an old party in a tattered picture hat. Across blanketed knees lay a rifle. The picture hat was a woman's, faded purple, decorated with bunches of wax grapes and cloth grape leaves, but the rider in the chair had a long white beard and long white hair.

"Mr. Brandstetter?" He twitched a smile of white dentures through the whiskers. "I'm sorry to have kept you waiting." He stopped the chair, peered fearfully through the gates, up and down the street, then set the rifle aside and began, with a rattle of keys, to undo padlocks that held thick chains in place where the two gates came together. "I have no one to help me right now. The television tells me constantly that unemployment today is a national disaster, yet no one seems to want to work."

"How much do you want to pay?" Dave asked.

"Ah-ha! You've put your finger on it, haven't you?" The last of the chains rattled and hung loose. "They think I'm rich." He scraped a key around on the lockplate of the gates. The hand that held the key was bones under dry, brown-spotted skin, and the hand was not steady. "They want ten dollars an hour, don't they? And if they can't have ten dollars an hour, they'd rather steal, thank you." Gifford cranked the key around in the lock. "I'm talking about the blacks, of course. The Hispanics already have jobs. They know what real hunger is. There are no food stamps in Mexico." Gifford caused the chair to move a couple of feet. His breath came in gasps as he dragged at something inside the gates. A bar. The sound of it said it was thick and heavy. "There, now." Gifford picked up the rifle and backed the chair out of the way. "Just push, please."

Dave pushed. Sirens went off. Bells clamored. The old man in the grape hat grinned and yelled something. Dave couldn't make it out. Gifford pointed a bony finger at the Jaguar. He made a summoning gesture with a skinny arm. Dave ran out to the car, got inside, fumbled to get the key into the ignition. He waited for Gifford to roll to the side of the drive, out of the way, then pulled the Jaguar through the gates. He jumped out of the car and ran to slam the gates shut. The sirens and the bells ceased. Except inside his head. Up at the house, the big dogs raved. Dave closed the padlocks on the chains, and slid the bar across. Gifford wheeled up and turned the key in the lock again.

"I'm not rich," he said. "No way in the world can I pay a servant eighty dollars a day. I'm lucky to have a roof over my head." He pushed his clump of keys into the pocket of a raveled brown cardigan sweater and turned the chair so that he faced Dave. "Mother always warned me I would someday regret my riotous youth. I do regret it—but not in the way she meant. I certainly do not regret the riotousness." The motor of the chair whined. It rolled up the drive toward the house that rose high and white among the trees. "I regret the days when I lacked the imagination to get up to anything riotous." He stopped the chair and half turned it back. "Come along. I'm delighted to have a visitor."

"It was good of you to call the Sheriff for me."

"I couldn't let anything happen to a car like that. My friend Ramon and I favored Jaguars in our time." Gifford's eyes were small and sunken but bright. "Ramon Novarro,

you know? Will it shock you if I tell you we were lovers?"
He looked Dave up and down. "That's Brooks Brothers,
isn't it?" He stated it as fact. It was a fact. He nodded. "Yes.
It suits you. You have a beautiful figure. When I saw you
stop on Lemon Street, I thought you were younger. There's
something young about your carriage, isn't there?" He
turned the chair abruptly and wheeled away up the drive
again. "What did you want at the Myers house? A lot of
strangers have been stopping there lately."

"Paul Myers died suddenly." Dave walked alongside the
wheelchair. "That usually brings strangers. I'm from the
company that insured his life. Do you know the names of
everyone in Gifford Gardens?"

"Paul Myers was witness two years ago to a supermarket
holdup." Gifford rolled the chair up the long, easy grade of
a wooden ramp to the spindlework verandah. Dave climbed
the stairs. He wondered about those big dogs barking inside the house. Gifford said, "He was on the television
news. That brought him to my attention." The house doors
were a pair, each with two tall, narrow panes of glass etched
with Pre-Raphaelite lotuses. Gifford pushed open the
doors. The dogs did not come bounding out. The dogs
stopped barking.

Gifford rolled his chair into a hallway spacious and two
stories high, where a broad, carved staircase climbed, to
divide left and right at a landing beneath a stained-glass
window. Dogs clawed, snuffled, growled behind closed
sliding doors. Dave followed the old man in the floppy
grape hat into a passageway beside the stairs. He glimpsed
a large, dim room with furniture under shrouds. Gifford
told him, "I used to entertain a good deal. Especially
when Mother was away in Europe. She didn' t take to my
friends." He bumped open a swinging door to a pantry pas-
sage. "Now that she's dead and out of the way, so are they."

He gave a brief hoot of irony. "Oh, my dear. What a joke life is."

He poked a black button in a brass wall plate. A metal door whose white enamel bore long horizontal scratches slid open. "This was once a dumbwaiter. The kitchen is below. I adored riding up and down in it as a little girl." He slid aside a folding metal grille. "When I lost the use of my legs, I had it converted." He gestured with the impatience of an old man irritated by his incapacities. "Get in, get in." Dave stepped into the cramped metal box, and Gifford backed his chair into it and rattled the grille shut. He poked a button, the steel door closed, the elevator jerked, thumped, began to rise. Slowly. Shivering. "That's a handsome young man staying at the Myers house," Gifford said. "I saw you talking to him. Who is he?"

"Mrs. Myers's kid brother," Dave said.

"I love it when they go around without their shirts."

"He's there to protect her," Dave said. "Somebody gave her a beating. She says it was her husband. I don't think so. A day or two before he was killed, did you see anyone stop there, any strangers? When Myers wasn't at home?"

"He was rarely at home." The elevator jerked to a halt and Gifford tugged back the folding grille. He pressed the button that worked the steel door. It slid back, and he rolled out of the elevator. "He was always off somewhere in that enormous truck of his. Often gone for days."

They had reached the attic, wide and high and gloomy. Also hot, though an air conditioner rattled someplace out of sight. With its quiet whine, the wheelchair took Gifford along a crooked aisle between heaps of packing cases, barrels, trunks thick with dust and cobwebs. Dave followed, dodging the corner of an old yellow life raft.

"Mind your head," Gifford said. "I should get rid of that. A young man who lived with me for a time after the war had survived on one of those for days after his ship was sunk in the South Pacific. Once, driving to the beach, he caught sight of that propped outside a surplus store. He got all nostalgic and simply had to have it. I bought it for him. Along with the compressed-air containers to inflate it. Absurd. Still, it made him sleep easier." Gifford sniffed. "Naturally, he left it behind when he decamped."

He rounded a chimney of rosy old brick and crusty mortar, and was in a cleared space that held a four-poster bed with a handsome patchwork spread, a chest of drawers with a cankered mirror, and a television set. On the wall was a blown-up photograph of Ramon Novarro, stripped to the waist and oiled. Off this space opened the tower room—couch, coffee table, wing chair. A pair of large, expensive binoculars stood on a windowsill. Gifford said, "A wife can grow weary of being left alone so much." He leaned the rifle against the chest, tossed the picture hat onto the bed. "No wonder she took a lover."

Dave stared. "Are you talking about Angela Myers?"

"Who else?" Gifford smoothed his uncut hair. He nodded. "Behind that partition"—he meant the one at the head of the bed—"you'll find a kitchen. I do all my living up here now. It's simpler. And cheaper. And the attic was always the most amusing part of the house. I spent much of my wretched childhood up here—the unwretched part. Old books, old magazines, old steamer trunks full of gowns and hats."

"You're sure about the lover?" Dave said. "Who is he?"

"I was trying to say"—Gifford struggled to get out of the frayed cardigan—"that it is hot up here, and a gin and tonic would be welcome, and would you fix it, please?"

"My pleasure." Dave found the kitchen in a sunny gable, everything neat and compact, stove, refrigerator, steel sink, cupboards, floor mopped and waxed. He found glasses. Gin, ice, and quinine water were in the refrigerator. He built the drinks while Gifford talked on.

"Wonderful, awful old books. I read them all, no matter how boring. There were tons of yellowback French novels, terribly naughty by *fin de siècle* standards. With a dictionary, I used them to teach myself French. And when reading palled, and dressing up, there were always these windows to watch out of. We were isolated out here in those days, but hikers came, and sometimes lovers. I saw some charming pastoral tableaux down among the oaks by the creek on warm summer days. At nights, I crept down for a closer look. That was how I learned anatomy and physiology. I was keen on self-education, you see. Naturally, I saw some things I ought never to have seen, and that haunt me still. But that is what little boys who prowl and spy upon others can expect, isn't it?"

"I couldn't locate any mint." Dave found Gifford in the tower room, seated in the wing chair, peering through the binoculars, frail fingers adjusting the focus. When he heard Dave, he set the glasses on the windowsill, sat back, smiled, held out his shaky hand to take the glass. "There is no mint, alas. In the kitchen garden, there used always to be mint. But that was long ago." He rattled the ice in his drink and sipped at it, dribbling bubbles into his beard. "Ah, delicious." He waved at a couch, Empire style, covered by a fringed Spanish shawl almost as threadbare as the upholstery it was meant to hide. "Sit down."

Dave continued to stand. "You know the man's name?"

"I make it a point to learn the names of people who interest me from afar. Bruce Kilgore. He operates a school down there, under the rubber tree." Gifford gestured vaguely. "I believe the generic term for them is white-flight schools."

"Right. How do you know they're lovers? There are no more oaks for them to make love under down by the creek."

Dave walked to the windows. They were shiny clean, inside and out. How did Gifford manage that? The view was amazing for distance and breadth. "Can you see her bedroom windows from here? Does she forget to lower the blinds?"

"You ask a good many questions for an insurance salesman," Gifford said, and his sunken eyes, bright and curious as a six-year-old's, fixed Dave from under brushy white brows. "That isn't what you are, really, is it?"

"I'm a death-claims investigator," Dave said. "When it looked as if Myers had an accident, the insurance company wasn't unduly worried. When it emerged that somebody blew his truck up with a bomb, they hired me."

"You didn't come here to thank me," Gifford said. "You came to pump me."

Dave gave him a thin smile. "One of the deputies who came in response to your telephone call about my car said you see everything that goes on in Gifford Gardens. You're obviously civic-minded. I assumed you'd want to help me."

Gifford studied him for what seemed a long time. He cleared his throat. "She didn't forget to pull the blinds. But he came only late at night, when the husband was away"— Gifford drank thirstily again—"and the children were almost certain to be asleep. What would you make of that?"

"And the night Myers was killed?"

A ledger lay on the coffee table, with stacks of magazines and books, a potted fern in supermarket green foil, an ashtray with a cigarette butt in it. Dave saw no cigarette pack on the table, nor on the stand by the bed, which held a lamp, a clock radio, a telephone, and another photograph of Ramon Novarro, this one in a tarnished silver frame. The ink of an inscription had faded. Gifford stretched a hand out for the ledger, laid it on his blanketed knees, turned pages covered with closely written ballpoint script. "Ah-ha. Here we are. Night of the ninth." Gifford smoothed the page. He sat straight. His eyesight must have been childlike too, un-blurred. "On that night, she was away. With the children. All night. Kilgore did not appear. Mrs. Myers reached home with the children about seven-forty-five. Sheriff's officers were waiting to give her the bad news." He closed the ledger and gave Dave a smug little nod. "I keep written records. The memory plays so many tricks."

"Thank you." Dave frowned. "You used the word 'came' about Kilgore. Is it over? Doesn't he come anymore?"

"Not since Myers died." Gifford shrugged. "After all, the beautiful brother is in the way, isn't he? But no, it is not over."

"They meet at Kilgore's, while the brother babysits?"

"Kilgore has living quarters at the school," Gifford said. "Yes, as you say. Twice, anyway. Perhaps more." He twitched a smile inside the frowsty beard. "After all, I am not King Argus of the Hundred Eyes, who never slept." His two creepy, clear child's eyes twinkled at Dave. "It will amuse you to learn that Mrs. Myers went straight to see Kilgore after she left the house this morning in her waitress's uniform, while you remained behind with the beautiful brother. What did you say his name was?"

"I didn't say. For what it's worth, it's Eugene Molloy." Dave nodded at the ledger. "No one came and beat Mrs. Myers up on the night of the ninth. When did they come? Who were they? Or were you sleeping?"

"It was two nights before." Gifford's hand strayed across the rough gray fabric of the ledger cover, as if to open the book again, but he didn't open it. He said, "I have my own reasons for remembering that night. It was well after dark. A stocky, middle-aged woman came, and two muscular men. She was startlingly well dressed. They, I think, were truck drivers. They arrived in a van without markings. I can't see license numbers at night. They didn't stay long. Five or ten minutes. When they came out, one of the men was rubbing his knuckles. The next day, when I got a glimpse of Mrs. Myers taking in some dry clothes from the backyard, her face was a mass of bruises, and she moved as if in pain."

"Never seen the stocky woman and her goons before?"

Gifford shook his head. "It wasn't her husband who beat her. Why do you suppose she told you that? He didn't come home that night, or all the next day until dusk. I gather he was moonlighting." Gifford laid the ledger back on the table. "Who was that handsome chap who arrived this morning while you were there? Spanish, right? What we might call 'a living doll,' might we not? What did he want?"

Dave told the old man who Jaime Salazar was. "He came to say they have a suspect in the murder of Paul Myers. A recent parolee named Silencio Ruiz." Gifford gasped and stiffened in his chair. Dave said, "Are you all right?"

"I live my life in pain," Gifford snapped. "So will you, when you're seventy-five." His voice was a wheeze, he gulped feebly and pointed. "If you don't mind? The bathroom? Digitalis."

A small bathroom backed the small kitchen. A dozen little amber plastic cylinders held pills in a medicine cabinet that also contained a pressure can of shaving cream and a pack of throwaway razors. Dave put on reading glasses and found the digitalis. He tapped a pill into his palm. A glass stood on the washbasin beside a box of denture cleaner. He filled the glass. In the tower room, trembling, the old man popped the pill into his mouth and gulped the water. He sat with eyes shut, panting. He whispered:

"Thank you. I won't keep you. The keys to the gates are

in my sweater." He fluttered a weak hand toward the bed. "When you've locked up, throw the keys as far up the drive as you can. I'll retrieve them later."

"Shouldn't I call your doctor and wait till he comes?"

"It's nothing. Happens all the time. It will pass. You're very kind." Gifford opened his eyes. They were cold. So was his voice. "Be careful on your way out of the house. My dogs are trained to kill." The coldness left. His smile was saintly. "Thank you for coming to see a boring old cripple. I hope I've been of some help."

"I appreciate it." Dave dug the keys from the ragged sweater, and found his way out. Carefully.

6

Chunky, hairy, tanned, Bruce Kilgore pedaled an Exercycle in one of three rooms at the back of the lot occupied by the Kilgore School. His black, sweaty hair was thinning, he wore blue jogging shorts and running shoes. Sitting straight, look-ma-no-hands style, he spooned yoghurt from a yellow paper cup. Outside an open sliding glass door, the children Dave had seen earlier, waiting by the front gate, kicked a black and white soccer ball around. Their voices were shrill. From the size of the exercise ground, Dave guessed that once there had been a swimming pool in its place. Had the buildings originally housed a motel? The rooms were uniform motel-unit size. The others he had peered into held school desks. This one had a big desk, file cabinets, telephones, bookcases, typewriter, home-size computer, framed certificates on the wall. Except for the Exercycle, it was unmistakably a school office. It was also unmistakably a motel room.

"I'd ride a ten-speed on the streets," Kilgore was saying by way of apology, "but the only ten-speeds you'll see in Gifford Gardens are the green ones that belong to the G-G's." He climbed off the machine and picked up a towel from a chair heaped with workbooks, wrapped reams of paper, a half-dozen boxed videotapes. "They're our local Ch cano gang." He set the yoghurt cup on a corner of hi paper-heaped desk, where the cup fell over and spilled it spoon. The spoon rattled on the floor. Kilgore ignored it and dried himself. "They discourage anyone else from riding bicycles. And if they weren't enough, there's our local black gang, The Edge."

"Tell me about it," Dave said. "They've already made a pass at my car radio and stolen my hubcaps." He leaned out the door for a look at the Jaguar at the curb. It was all right. For the moment. "And I've only been in town for a few hours."

"In Edge territory." Kilgore threw the towel over the Exercycle and pulled on sweatpants, having a little trouble with the elastic at the cuffs getting caught on the jogging shoes. "The way they've laid out this community puts political gerrymandering to shame. 'Turf' they call the parts they rule. By terror. You never know where you are—not for long. The boundaries keep shifting. There are continual skirmishes. It's like the Middle East." He went to the door, blew a steel whistle, and called, "Okay. Time's up. Back to class. Don't leave the ball there. Somebody will climb in and steal it." He waited and watched, the whistle dangling its black leather thong from his mouth, while the youngsters funneled back into school. The last to go was Brian Myers, head hanging, with its shock of fair hair. Hands jammed into pockets, he scuffed his feet. Kilgore called, "Brian—you okay?"

The boy halted, turned, gave a wan smile. "I'm okay, Mr. Kilgore." He went on through an open glass sliding door into the school. One of the gray striped cats bumped his legs, looked up at him, meowed. He bent and petted it for a minute. Then he glanced back at Kilgore across the empty yard, stood, and went on out of sight, still dragging his feet.

"Poor kid," Kilgore said mechanically, returning to his desk, sitting down behind it, tossing the whistle into the litter there. "Just lost his dad."

"Paul Myers." Dave glanced at the Jaguar one more time, where it waited beyond the side gate. He came inside the office and walked to the desk. "It's about him that I've come." He laid his card in front of Kilgore. "Mrs. Myers was here earlier. I presume she told you what happened to her husband was no accident. That somebody blew him up with a bomb planted in his truck."

Kilgore stared. His tan turned putty color. "Silencio Ruiz, but how did you—" He half stood up, and sat down again as if he hadn't strength in those muscular brown legs of his. "Who told you she came here?"

"You're close friends," Dave said. "It's no secret. You've been close friends for some time. The kind of close friends who visit one another late at night when the husband is away at work."

Kilgore's color darkened. Veins stood out in his short, thick neck. "It's a lie. Your implication is a lie. Yes, I visit late at night. Look at this." He spread his hands, palms up, above the cluttered desk. "You think I've got help around here? Think again. The last thing I am is principal of a school. I don't know what comes first—janitor, accountant, secretary, fund-raiser, teacher? You decide. When the hell else do I have time to visit but late at night?" He picked up the card, glared at it, glared at Dave. "What business is it of yours, anyway?"

"Maybe none," Dave said. "I don't know yet. If it has something to do with Paul Myers's death, it's important, isn't it? With what happened to him, why it happened, and who was behind it?"

"What do you mean?" Kilgore licked his lips. "Myers appreciated my looking in on his family. He had to be out of town a lot. He was a cross-country trucker. If he was going to earn a living, he had to leave them here, unprotected. And that's not a figure of speech, either. After his testimony put Silencio Ruiz in jail, the G-G's harassed them night and day. Ruiz was their leader."

"Mrs. Myers told me," Dave said. "She didn't tell me it was you who made them stop."

"First I tried the Sheriff." Kilgore dug among the disorder on his desk, found a handball, and began squeezing it. He snorted. "Fat lot of good that did. Even after they smashed the windows, even after they shot the dog, the Sheriff wouldn't put a guard on the house. Didn't have the manpower, they said." He switched the ball to his other hand and squeezed. Muscles showed in his forearm. "Then they started this program to get the gangs off the streets. They enlisted businesses, banks, churches, to start basketball teams, figuring the G-G's and The Edge would get the same kick out of slamdunking as they do out of slaughtering each other with guns and knives and bicycle chains." His laugh was sour. "It didn't work, of course. I mean, you know what we're talking about here—subhumans, primitives, savages. Jungle warfare. It's in their blood, right?"

Dave said wearily, "Is there a point to this?"

"There's a rich old geezer out here," Kilgore said. "Maybe you've seen his house. The old mansion on the hill with all the gingerbread work? De Witt Gifford. And this is the interesting part—he donated the jackets for one of the basketball teams. The Gifford Gardens gang, the Latinos. There's no team anymore, but they still wear the jackets."

"I've seen them. What's interesting about it?"

"It didn't add up. He never contributes anything to this community—not a dime. It's named after his family, but he doesn't give a damn what happens to it or anybody in it.

46

So why the jackets for the G-G's? I began nosing around, asking questions. About Silencio Ruiz's trial. Now, normally he'd have had a public defender, right? And normally he'd never have made bail. He'd have sat behind bars for months, waiting for his day in court. Well, he didn't. He made bail. And he had an expensive attorney. At first everybody kept their mouths shut. They'd been paid to. That's what I figured. So I shelled out a little money myself. And guess what I found out?"

"Gifford put up the bail and paid the lawyer. You mean you used this to get him to make the G-G's quit harassing the Myerses? Seriously? He worried about it being known? At his age? In his condition?"

"He was scared to death." Kilgore flipped the handball into an empty metal wastebasket across the room. "I only went to him on a hunch. I was surprised as hell when it worked. He panicked. Gave me a five-hundred-dollar check for the school, and made me promise I wouldn't tell anybody about him helping Silencio."

"You're telling me," Dave said.

"All bets are off now," Kilgore said. "Silencio killed Myers. The minute he got out of prison. Gifford didn't prevent that, did he? It was him who told you I was seeing Mrs. Myers late at night, wasn't it? He spies from one of those towers up there. Everybody knows it. He hates me because I won't let Latinos in my school. Crazy old bastard. He wears dresses—did you know that?"

"Mrs. Myers has her brother to guard her now," Dave said, "but you still see each other at night. Only now she comes to you. What about? The children's grades?"

"I don't have to answer your questions." Kilgore got to his feet without trouble this time. "Get out of here."

"Paul Myers doesn't care if you're sleeping with his

wife—not anymore. Neither do I. If that's all you have to hide, why not answer my questions?"

"You care. You're implying collusion between us—me and Angie—Mrs. Myers, I mean."

Dave raised his brows. "Am I?" He went to look out the door at the Jaguar again. No crime in progress. He turned back. "You mean I think you murdered Myers so as to marry his widow and share in the insurance money?" Dave gestured to indicate the school and its burdens. "You're hard up. A hundred thousand dollars would hire a lot of help. No? You could ride your exercise machine all day."

"Silencio Ruiz killed Myers," Kilgore said.

"There are reasons to doubt that," Dave said. "Where were you on the night Myers crashed and burned? You didn't visit Angela Myers that night."

"She was at her parents' house," Kilgore said. "Her mother needed her. The old man was acting up. She took the children and stayed there overnight."

"And where did you stay?"

"Right the hell here," Kilgore said. "And no, I can't prove it." He came from behind the desk, fists bunched. "And I don't have to prove it. Not to you. I know what you're doing. Trying to link Angie to Paul's death so your company doesn't have to pay. And you think you can get to her through our relation—through me. Well, the hell with you, mister. Just leave, all right? I'm warning you."

Dave pointed to the wall. "That certificate says you graduated from the California School of Engineering. Did they teach you how to wire up an explosive device? And detonate it by remote control?"

Kilgore narrowed his eyes. "Do you carry a gun?"

"I'm licensed to carry a gun." Dave smiled. "Why do you ask?"

"Because if you haven't got a gun on you," Kilgore said, "I'm going to beat the shit out of you."

"Not bright," Dave said. "It would draw adverse attention to your school. And the Sheriff's department would wonder about your overreaction to a few harmless questions. Also"—he smiled again, and patted his ribs on the left side where a holster would be if he owned a holster, if he owned a gun to put into a holster—"maybe I have a gun. What was Myers hauling in his semi at night up in that canyon?"

Kilgore looked sulky. "How the hell should I know?"

"Angie Myers doesn't know either." Dave lit a cigarette. "Neither of you gave a damn about Paul Myers, did you? You had each other, after all."

"Don't smoke in here," Kilgore said.

Dave said, "I'm leaving in a minute. She was beaten up about the time he was killed. That must have upset you, caring for her as you do. How did it happen? Who did it to her?"

Kilgore went back to his desk but didn't sit down. "She wouldn't say." He picked up a stack of unopened envelopes and sorted through them, frowning. "Why wasn't it Paul? He was nothing but a truck driver, after all."

"You seem ready with your fists, yourself," Dave said.

"And your face doesn't look marked." Kilgore let the envelopes fall. "Which is remarkable, considering the things you say to perfect strangers."

"Nobody's perfect," Dave said.

A voice called across the play area. "Mr. Kilgore?" Kilgore muttered impatiently, rounded the desk, passed Dave. A fragile-looking young woman in big tinted spectacles stood in the open doorway of the complex under the rubber tree. Red paint had splashed the front of her skirt. "I've got a mini-riot." She sounded on the edge of tears. "Can you settle it, please?" Kilgore sighed and jogged across the sunlit space. The two of them vanished into the building.

Dave left the office. He tried the door of the unit next to it. The door opened. At the rear of the room was a kitchenette with a breakfast bar and two stools. At the front stood a chair and a two-seater sofa in tough green and tan plaid. A low table held books, magazines, and two empty coffee mugs, one marked with lipstick. Stereo components occupied modular shelves that also held records. A door stood open to a bathroom. Dave went just far enough into the larger room to see that the bathroom had a door on its other side. This too stood partway open. And beyond it he glimpsed, in a band of sunlight, an unmade bed and the corner of a television set. He stepped outside again, pulled the door shut, and went quietly away.

7

Terence Molloy wore a new bathrobe but food had spilled down it and dried. He stood clutching the shiny bars of a walker, and screwed up his face against the bright hot daylight outside the screen door. His face was twisted anyway, mouth drooping at the left corner, left eyelid drooping. His thick gray hair had been slicked down with water, but his beard was bristly—he'd gone a couple of days without a shave.

He croaked, "Who are you? What do you want?"

Dave gave his name and stated his business. "I'm sorry to bother you, Mr. Molloy. I know you're not well. Is your wife at home?"

The street of clipped hedges and Spanish-style bungalows was quiet. Dave heard a toilet flush inside the house, heard footsteps hurrying. Faith Molloy appeared, a dumpy woman in a faded house dress. Molded shoes made her feet look big. Above them, her ankles were swollen. "It says no salesmen or solicitors."

Her husband said, "You don't know what you're talking about. It's about Paul. You always go off half-cocked." He hiked the walker forward and fumbled with a trembling hand at the screen-door latch. "Come in."

"Oh, sure," Faith Molloy said. "I haven't got anything to do but entertain strangers."

"I won't be long." Dave pulled open the screen door and stepped inside. He told the old man, "Thank you."

"Go crazy around here with only her for company," Terence Molloy said. "My glad-hearted colleen. Look at her. Face like a sour apple."

"He's not himself," Faith Molloy said.

"On the night Paul died," Dave said, "did Angela bring the children and stay here with you?"

"I needed her. This one was acting up. Of course, I needed two more children. A sixty-five-year-old one isn't enough." Faith Molloy snatched up scattered sections of the morning *Times*. The furniture was puffy overstuffed covered in a yellow and pink flower print. She kneed the Off button of a television set. A game show quit in the middle. "Sit down. I suppose you'll be wanting coffee?"

"Not if it's any trouble." Dave sat on the sofa.

"I wouldn't know how to handle it, if it wasn't trouble." She went away with the crumpled newspaper.

Dave asked the old man, "Paul was working nights so he could help you out financially. Do you know what he was hauling, who he was working for?"

"He never said." The old man shuffled in his shiny rack to the easychair that faced the television set. "And I wasn't about to pry. None of my business." He threw Dave a warning scowl. "No, don't get up and help me, God damn it. I can manage." He wangled the rack into position and dropped onto the sagging cushions. With his good foot, in a fake leather bedroom slipper, he pushed the rack clumsily aside. "Going to miss Paul. He was a real son to me."

"Where was Gene that night?" Dave said.

"He's over there, isn't he? At Angie's? That's where you come from, I suppose." Terence Molloy looked at the small table beside his chair. The lamp was painted china with a fluted shade. Under it clustered pill containers and medicine bottles. He frowned. Then he began poking with his hand down between the chair arm and the cushion. He came up with a round snuff can, fidgeted it open, tucked snuff into his cheek. He looked anxiously over his shoulder, closed the can, tossed it to Dave. "Hide that. They want you to relax, but anything that would relax you—tobacco, booze—you can't have those."

Dave pushed the can under the sofa cushion. "Where was Gene? Here?"

"I wouldn't let him through that door. Living off some woman, probably. His mother spoiled hell out of him. Angie always had a soft spot in her head for him. You watch, he'll live off her the rest of his useless life."

"She seems to know how to handle him," Dave said.

Terence Molloy snorted. "He's there, isn't he? And Paul not cold in his grave."

"It wouldn't be worth it to him for her wages as a waitress," Dave said. "She'll barely make ends meet that way for herself and the kids."

The old man's attention wasn't on him. He was staring blankly, slack-jawed, at the blank television screen. His nails needed trimming. With them, he was plucking at his beard stubble. Under his breath, he sang, quavery and off-key. Some old Irish song. "'And in all me life I ne'er did see such a foin young girl, upon my soul . . .'" He looked at Dave with sudden sharpness, and said, "It's for the insurance money. That's what you're thinking, isn't it? You said you were from the insurance company."

"It will be a lot of money if it's paid," Dave said. "Would Gene be sure enough of Angie's taking him in to cause Paul to have an accident that would get him out of the way so he, Gene, could live happily ever after on the insurance?"

The old man stared, mouth open. "Are you saying it wasn't an accident?"

Dave told him what it was.

Faith Molloy came in with coffee in a cup and saucer, and bent to set it on a little table at Dave's elbow. "Who would do such a thing?"

"I was wondering if it could be Gene," Dave said.

Still half bent above the table, face close to the lampshade, white as the lampshade, Faith Molloy went still. For a moment her face was expressionless. Dave could see where Gene's good looks came from. She must have been a beauty, forty years ago. At last she found her voice, enough to whisper, "Gene?"

"It would be a fitting end," the old man said. "The hangman's noose."

The woman turned on him in fury. "He never harmed anyone in his life. He's weak, that's all. He'd never hurt anybody." She looked at Dave. "It isn't in him."

"Weak? He's a liar, a thief, a gambler, a drunk, and a lecher. No morals. No scruples. No self-respect. What did you expect, woman?"

"You shut your crazy old mouth." Faith Molloy screamed this. She turned frantically to Dave. "Don't listen to him. He's sick. His mind's gone. Half the time he doesn't know his own name."

"Gene's at your daughter's now," Dave said. "Where was he living before?"

"I've got it written down." She threw a savage look at her husband and left the room, muttering, "You wicked old devil. Your only son. Your flesh and blood. Name of your name."

Terence Molloy picked up a metal crutch from beside his chair, reached out, and with its rubber tip pulled the television button. The game show returned. Gold curtains flew open. A new blue automobile gleamed on a turntable. A young red-haired woman in green jumped up and down with joy and hugged the wrinkled MC, who raised his eyebrows in simulated surprise. Terence Molloy let the crutch fall. "I'd beat her with that," he said, "if I had the strength. I was a strong man once. She wouldn't have dared plague me then as she does now. Now all I can do to her is spill my food and piss in the bed."

"Here it is." Faith Molloy came hurrying back in her clumsy shoes and pushed a scrap of paper into Dave's hand. "Gene has a lot of friends. He'll have been with his friends. He likes to have a good time. They'll have seen him that night. They'll tell you."

"Thank you." Folding the paper, tucking it away, Dave got off the sagging couch. "There's nothing to worry about, then, is there?"

"Oh, my dear man." She shook her head despairingly. "I hope you never know how much there is to worry about."

"If you'd be quiet," the old man said, "I could hear the television. This man doesn't want to know your troubles. People have troubles of their own."

Dave moved toward the open front door, the screen with the sunlight glaring on it. Faith Molloy tagged after him and plucked his sleeve. "You won't stop the insurance coming, will you?"

"Not I," Dave said.

"Paul told us we wouldn't have to worry if anything happened to him. He'd bought a hundred thousand dollars worth of insurance, and we were to get half."

"He sounds like a good man," Dave said.

"Oh, he was. Why is it the awful ones go on and on living?" She turned to glare at her husband. "Why does Our Lord always take the good?"

"Because nobody on earth deserves them," the old man

shouted over the television racket. "No woman—that's for sure."

The building was two-story brown brick, on a Hollywood corner opposite two filling stations and a hamburger shack with a tin sign: BIGGIE'S. Downstairs, the brown brick building housed a bar called Liza's, with caricatures painted on its windows of a young woman with wide eyes, scarlet mouth, long black gloves, champagne glass in one hand, long cigarette holder in the other.

Down the side street, near the back corner of the building, Dave found a door whose beveled glass bore the address that Faith Molloy had given him. He climbed narrow, newly carpeted stairs to a hallway of old closed doors. The air was hot and smelled of room deodorant. At the far end of the hallway, a window showed a slatted iron fire escape. But the inspectors hadn't been here lately; across the window, shelves held trailing philodendrons.

Dave knocked on door number three. Music thumped up from the bar below, but no sound came from beyond the door. He knocked again. A door down the hall opened and a tall, reedy man stepped out. He wore an apron, short shorts, and cowboy boots, and he had a small gold ring in one ear. His hair ought to have been gray but it was strawberry color, upswept, shiny. In one scrawny arm he cradled a brown Mexican pottery bowl. It held yellow batter that he was whipping with a wooden spoon.

He said, "You're too late, darling. The hunk has flown."

"Gene Molloy?" Dave said. "You a friend of his?"

The man shook his head. The strawberry curls quivered. "He didn't have boyfriends; he had girlfriends." The man let go of the spoon, laid the back of a hand against his forehead, sighed. "God knows, I tried. But that old green taffeta just doesn't fool them anymore."

56

Dave grinned. "I thought he lived with somebody."

"*Off* somebody. Liza. You'll find her downstairs. She'll be the one gnashing her teeth. I've warned her it'll play hell with those mail-order dentures, but women are so emotional." He lifted the spoon and critically watched the batter run off it. "Look, I have to get this in the oven. My God, it's hot. I'm dying for a drink. How about you?"

"I'll die a little longer, thanks. Would you know—was he around here on the night of the ninth?"

The man turned his head, watched out of the corners of his eyes. "That was the night he smashed up the bar. But you already knew that, didn't you?"

"Late or early?" Dave said.

"Late—one o'clock. It was just Irish high spirits, but Liza got hysterical and called the cops."

"Did they arrest him, book him, lock him up?"

"All night. But Liza bailed him out next morning."

"He brought the body here in his own car," Cole Wrightwood said. A plump, sleek black, he wore a dark pinstripe suit, a quiet tie, and a large diamond ring. The desktop in front of him was polished to a high gloss. Along its front edge in a planter grew a neat low hedge of marigolds. In corners of the paneled office, tall white baskets held sprays of gladioluses. The cool conditioned air was laden with the damp perfume of flowers. Electronic organ music—Fauré? Widor?—whispered from hidden loudspeakers. "And waited while I filled out the death certificate. As I expect you know"—Wrightwood smiled a grave, apologetic little smile—"the mortician fills in all the data—name, address, that sort of thing. The physician merely has to write in the cause of death and sign the certificate."

"He has to have been the attending physician," Dave said, "for at least twenty days. Otherwise there has to be an

57

autopsy. The word of a man called in just for the emergency isn't enough."

Wrightwood nodded. "The departed's wife, widow—she came along with the doctor. She said he was the family physician."

"Did that seem likely to you? White, isn't he?" A leaded window, diamond panes, churchlike, was at Wrightwood's back. A long, glossy Cadillac hearse slid past the window. "Had you ever seen him before?"

"He was white." Wrightwood's smile was thin. "Most doctors are. I saw no reason to doubt the woman's word. She was in tears, deeply grieved, shocked. In my experience, people don't lie at times like that."

"May I see the death certificate?"

Wrightwood stirred in his tall leather chair, but he didn't rise. "You say Oswald Bishop was insured by this company you represent?" The card Dave had given him lay on the desktop. He blinked at it through large round lenses framed in heavy black plastic. "Pinnacle?"

"I didn't say." Dave took from inside his jacket the leather folder that held his private investigator's license, and held it out across the marigolds for Wrightwood to read. "Pinnacle has asked me to investigate the death of a close friend of Ossie Bishop." He flipped the folder closed and slid it back into his jacket. "Another gypsy trucker. Paul Myers."

Wrightwood's eyebrows rose. "That was on the news. An accident. He drove off the road in some canyon."

"No." Dave told him what the Sheriff's lab had discovered. "Now, Ossie Bishop was doing the same sort of night-work as Myers. He even got Myers the job. His death coming so close to Myers's disturbs me." Dave smiled. "I'll regard it as a great kindness if you'll let me see Bishop's death certificate."

"What was this nightwork?"

"I don't know. You say Mrs. Bishop was distraught that night. She didn't happen to say—didn't blurt it out in anger or despair, perhaps?"

"You mean you don't know what these two men were doing with their trucks? Not even the one you insured?"

"Myers seems not to have told anyone. That in itself isn't exactly reassuring, is it? Not when you add the fact that he was very well paid." Dave took out Myers's bankbook and held it up. "He was making frequent fat deposits. In cash." He put the bankbook away.

Wrightwood sat for a few seconds longer, moving his chair very slightly from side to side on its swivel base. He shrugged and rose. "It was a heart attack." He rounded the desk, crossed deep purple carpeting, opened one of a pair of tall, carved, double doors. Through the doorway came the quiet chatter of a typewriter. Wrightwood spoke. The typewriter ceased. Branches of firethorn showed outside the window. Small birds were harvesting the berries, their squabbling shrill beyond the panes. Wrightwood returned and handed Dave a manila folder marked BISHOP, OSWALD B., with a date a month old.

Dave put on reading glasses and opened the folder. The shadow of Wrightwood came between him and the window light. The cushion of the big desk chair sighed as Wrightwood's two hundred sleek pounds settled on it. Written after CAUSE OF DEATH was *Massive coronary occlusion*. TIME OF DEATH: 1:50 A.M. ATTENDING PHYSICIAN: Ford T. Kretschmer, M.D. Kretschmer had written down an address and telephone number. Dave took off the glasses, folded them, pushed them into a pocket, closed the file, handed it across the sunny little flowers to Wrightwood. "Thank you." He got to his feet. "I appreciate it."

"It's on file at the Hall of Records."

"You were nearer," Dave said. "I'm sorry for the trouble. Anyway, you've told me things they couldn't at the Hall of Records."

Wrightwood turned his head slightly, wary. "It was a heart attack. Big, heavy man. He'd overworked himself." Wrightwood got to his feet, buttoned his jacket. He didn't appear worried about his own weight. "Hypertension kills a good many of my people. I see men who have gone down in their prime all the time." He had come around the desk again, and now took Dave's arm to walk him to the door. His grip was as gentle and comforting as if Dave had just brought him a dead friend. "You interest me." He didn't let go Dave's arm. With his free hand he gripped the fancily wrought bronze handle of the tall office door, but he didn't move it. "Just what have I told you besides the obvious?"

"That the widow came here." Dave didn't want a cigarette, but he wanted the undertaker's hand off his arm. Nobody was dead around him—he didn't want to be treated as if somebody was. So he reached for a cigarette, found it, found his slim steel lighter, lit the cigarette. "Did the oldest son come too? Melvil?" He put the lighter away.

Wrightwood shook his head. "A woman came. I assumed she was a nurse—perhaps the doctor's receptionist."

"What made you think that?"

Wrightwood turned the handle and opened the door. "She fit the role. You develop an instinct about people in this business. She had that self-assured way about her. They boss their bosses." They were in a quiet reception room now. He gave the slim, pale black, fortyish woman at the desk a grin. "Don't they?"

She looked up at him, wide-eyed, and patted her beautifully set hair. "I can't think what you're talking about." Her laugh was soft and dry.

Dave smiled at her and moved toward the doors that

would take him along a hushed corridor hung with ferns and caged canaries, a corridor that passed rooms where the embalmed dead slept in coffins, rooms where damp-eyed families sat on spindly chairs, and past the chapel. It was the route he had taken to get here. With the door open, he turned back. "Can you describe her for me? Stocky, middle-aged, well-dressed?"

Wrightwood tilted his head. "You know this woman?"

"Not yet," Dave said. "But I'm looking forward to it. Thanks for your help."

8

The place he lived in had, he judged, started life as riding stables. He left the Jaguar beside Cecil's van, walked past the end of the long, shingle-sided front building, crossed the uneven bricks of a courtyard sheltered by an old oak. He unwrapped and laid on plates in the cookshack pastrami sandwiches he'd picked up on Fairfax, built Bloody Marys, and carried these on a bent-wood tray across to the long, shingle-sided rear building. The arrangement of the place was awkward, but it amused more than bothered him. The last of his dead father's nine beautiful wives, Amanda, had made the buildings hand-some and livable inside. If, during the short winter, getting from one building to another meant being soaked by rain or chilled by wind, novelty was on its side. It was never boring.

The back building was walled in knotty pine. There was a wide fireplace. The inside planking of the pitched roof showed, and the unpainted rafters. Above, Amanda had de-signed a sleeping loft. Climbing the raw pine steps to it now meant climbing into heat. The smell of sun-baked pine overlaid the old, almost forgotten smell of horse and hay that always ghosted the place. Cecil sat naked, propped black against white pillows, in the wide bed, sheet across his long, lean legs. He gleamed with sweat. His collarbone and ribs showed. Dave kept trying to fatten him up. It didn't seem to be working.

"Hey." Cecil tossed aside the latest *Newsweek* and smiled. "How was Gifford Gardens?"

"Words fail me." Dave set the tray on the long raw pine chest of drawers, carried his glass to Cecil, bent and kissed his mouth. "How are you?"

"I rested, like you told me," Cecil said. "Nearly driving me crazy." With a wry little smile, he raised his glass. "Cheers," he said cheerlessly, and drank.

Dave tasted his drink, then brought the sandwiches and napkins. He sat on the edge of the bed. "It's a little bit racist out there. Eat that. They also have gangs." He bit into his sandwich. That was the best delicatessen in L.A. When he'd washed the bite down with Bloody Mary, he said, "Can I borrow your van tomorrow?"

"Something happen to the Jag?" Cecil looked alarmed.

Dave told him what had happened to the Jag.

"Aw, no. Shit. It's my fault. I heard the kind of place it was, when I worked for Channel Three News." Cecil shook his head slowly in self-disgust. "I should have warned you."

"I wouldn't have taken you seriously." Dave set his plate on the bed and shed his jacket. "The place is beyond belief. Next time I'll drive a junk heap."

"Next time, just don't go," Cecil said. "Wonder is you came back with a car at all. Wonder is you came back alive. That is a killing ground out there. Grannies, little children, policemen." Cecil stretched out a long, skinny arm to take the cigarette pack from Dave's jacket where it lay on the bed. "I should have been with you."

"You're not supposed to smoke," Dave said. On a deadly night of rain last winter, in the lost back reaches of Yucca Canyon, flames leaping high from a burning cabin, bullets had punctured the boy's lungs. Cecil acted as if he hadn't heard. He lit the cigarette with Dave's lighter, and choked on the smoke. Coughing bent him forward, shook him. "Damn." He wiped away tears with his knuckles. "Damn."

Dave took the cigarette from him, stubbed it out in the bedside ashtray. "That'll larn you," he said.

For a moment, Cecil got the coughing under control. Eyes wet, voice a wheeze, he asked, "Where you going tomorrow? Where you taking my van?"

"San Diego County," Dave said. "And no, you can't go. It's too far. Look, will you please eat?"

Cecil coughed again, fist to mouth. When he finished, he picked up the sandwich. Wearily obedient, he bit into it. With his mouth full, he said, "Seem to me, if you take my van, it's only fair you take me." He gulped Bloody Mary, wiped tomato juice off his chin with the napkin. "Dave, I can't eat this. I'm not hungry." He laid the sandwich on the plate. His eyes begged. "I'm sorry. Maybe later."

"Right." Dave knew his smile was stiff, mechanical, false. He was growing discouraged. And frightened. "I'll wrap it in plastic and put it in the fridge. Don't forget it, now, okay?" Cecil nodded mutely and handed him the plate as if looking at it was more than he could bear. Dave rose and set it on the tray. He turned back. "I'll take you tomorrow, if you promise me something." The rear of the van was lushly carpeted—floor, walls, ceiling—in electric blue to contrast with the flame colors of the custom paint job. Picture window. Built-in bar, refrigerator, drop-leaf table. Electric blue easy chair. Electric blue wraparound couch. "You lie down. All the way."

Cecil made a face. He poked grumpily at the ice cubes in his Bloody Mary with a finger. He licked the finger, tried for a smile, and almost managed it. "Okay. I promise." He livened up a little. "Why are we going?"

"The reasons keep piling up." Dave sat on the bed again, worked on his sandwich and drink, and reviewed the morning's events for Cecil. He finished, "So I went to see Dr. Ford Kretschmer. Only his address is a storage lot for galvanized pipe. And the telephone number is out of service."

Cecil stared. "He wasn't a doctor at all?"

"Maybe not." Sandwich and drink finished, Dave wiped fingers and mouth with his napkin, took Cecil's empty glass and his own with his plate to the tray on the chest. "Whoever he was, the woman with him was no nurse. She was the same one who showed up with goons at the Myers house three weeks later."

"The ones who beat her up?" Cecil said.

"You've got it." Dave picked up his jacket and shrugged into it. "I have to take the Jaguar down to the agency so they can replace that window." He dug from the jacket pocket the crumpled flimsies he had taken from the drawer under Paul Myers's bedroom closet. He hesitated. "You want to rest while I'm gone, or you want to do some work?"

Cecil reached for the papers. "Busy hands," he said, "are happy hands." He began separating the papers, frowning at them. "What are these? What do I do?"

"Telephone those companies. Get hold of whoever is in charge of shipping. Get out of them, if you can, whether Paul Myers was hauling anything except what's listed on those manifests. What did they think of Myers? Did any of them know him? If so, did they know who he was moonlighting for, what he was hauling? Anything, everything."

"Do I pretend I'm you again?" Cecil said.

Dave grinned. "If it's not too much of a strain on your natural femininity."

Cecil threw a pillow at him.

Dave laughed and carried the tray down the stairs.

On sun-scorched lots where weeds grew through the asphalt, and faded plastic pennons fluttered from sagging wires overhead, he looked at battered cars not quite but almost ready for the junkyard. Two or three he test-drove. They bucked and gasped through trash-blown neighborhoods of desolate lumberyards, warehouses, and shacky motels, while salesmen in polyester doubleknit suits breathed mouthwash fumes beside him, lying about mileage, lifetime batteries, and recent overhauls. In the end, he escaped Culver City in a 1969 two-door Valiant. A sideswipe had creased it deeply from front to back. Its crackly plastic upholstery leaked stuffing. But its gears worked, the engine ran smoothly, and the tires still had treads. It was a vague beige color, a hole gaped where its radio had been, and Dave pried loose and handed to the surprised salesman its one remaining hubcap before he drove off. The car labored up the canyon, but it didn't overheat. And when he left it parked on the leaf-strewn bricks of his tree-shady yard where the Jaguar customarily stood, he felt good. No one in Gifford Gardens would give this car a second look.

This time he fixed double martinis in the cookshack. And when he carried them into the rear building, music was in the air—Miles Davis, "Sketches of Spain." The ice in the hefty glasses jingled as he carried them up the stairs. The flimsies in their pale pinks, blues, yellows, lay spread out on the sheet across Cecil's legs. He told the telephone receiver "thank you" and put it back in its cradle. He reached for the martini and gave his beautiful head with its short-cropped hair a rueful shake.

"Not one of these companies shipped anything with Paul Myers but what's listed on these manifests." He patted the papers. "They all liked him. He was reliable, friendly, intelligent." Cecil sipped the martini, hummed, and for a moment shut his eyes in unwordable appreciation. "They are all sorry he's dead, but nobody can guess what he was hauling at night up in that canyon before he crashed." Cecil held the glass up in a salute to Dave, who was shedding his sweaty clothes. "You came back just in time. I was about to die of temperance up here, all alone by the telephone."

"Sorry about that, but when you hear what I've done, you'll be proud of me." Dave sat on the foot of the bed, perched his drink on the loft railing, shed shoes and socks. "I bought a jalopy to drive in Gifford Gardens. A genuine eyesore." He tried his martini. Better than usual. Most things were, now that Cecil was with him. "When you chance to pass it, avert your gaze, all right?"

"I can't promise." Cecil gathered up the flimsies. They crackled and whispered together. "Morbid fascination may be too much for me. How did you force yourself to commit this act of sound common sense?"

"I had the man at the Jaguar showroom in Beverly Hills run me over to the used-car lots on Washington in Culver City. You should have seen his expression. He couldn't believe the place." Dave hiked his butt and shed his trousers. He stood, holding the trousers up to get the creases straight. "The poor man kept repeating that he'd furnish me with a loaner until the window was fixed. I didn't have to do this desperate thing. He was almost in tears." Dave took down a wooden hanger from a wide knotty-pine wardrobe, and hung the pants on it. "But I was firm." He retrieved his jacket from where he'd draped it over the rail, and hung that on the hanger too. "If I made him strand me there, I'd have to buy wheels to get home on, wouldn't I?" He hung the suit in the wardrobe. It was damp with sweat and must go to the cleaners, but that could wait. What would he wear to Gifford Gardens next time? A raveled sweater and an old picture hat? He closed the wardrobe

doors. "I knew nothing less would force me into it." He
went to get his drink and saw Cecil watching him soberly
and big-eyed over the rim of his martini glass. "What's the
matter?"

"You saying it's going to get you to San Diego County?
You don't need my van, so you don't need me?"

"I'll be stretching my luck if it gets me to Gifford Gardens and back." Dave took off his tie, unbuttoned his shirt,
picked up his glass, sat on the bed. He put a hand on
Cecil's thigh. Too thin. "No, if you feel up to it at five tomorrow morning, we'll go in the van, the two of us." He
smiled. "I know I sound like the witch in the wood, but
what will you eat for supper that's fattening?"

Cecil's eyes brimmed with tears. "Man, I am so tired of
being sick and weak and no good to you and skinny and
ugly and full of scars. I am so tired of that."

"Hey," Dave said. The boy was weeping, and Dave took
the glass out of his hand. "If you're going to turn into a
maudlin drunk, I'll have to put you on Perrier water. And
there are no calories in that." He pulled tissues from a box
by the clock and the lamp. He dried Cecil's face and kissed
his salty mouth. "Come on, cheer up. You're home. That
means you're going to get well. All it needs is time. I'm
glad you're home. Aren't you glad you're home? If the answer is yes, smile."

Cecil worked up a forlorn smile. It didn't last. "Burden
on you," he said gloomily. "I didn't come back to you for
that."

"You didn't come back to me to get shot up, either,"
Dave said. "How do you suppose I feel about that?"

"Comes with the territory." This time there was some
conviction to Cecil's smile. He reached out. "Give me back
my strengthening medicine."

Dave put the glass in his hand. "I need a shower. You think you can wait here and not cry anymore?"

Cecil read the big black watch bristly with stops on his skeletal wrist. Miles Davis's thoughtful trumpet had gone silent. "Time for the news." Cecil nodded at the television set on the far side of the bed. "How can I cry, with all the happiness they are going to spread out for me, in all the colors of the rainbow?" He groped around in the bed for the remote switch. The set came on.

The picture was file film—of a charred eighteen-wheeler lying on its top in a canyon among blackened rocks and scorched brush. The big tires of the truck still smoked. Men in yellow hardhats and rubber suits crunched around the wreckage. High above, fire vehicles and a wrecking truck stood at the edge of a cliff road. Sheriff's cars. A television reporter's voice came through the speaker.

". . . but today, Sheriff's investigators revealed that the semi, owned and driven by independent trucker Paul Myers, thirty-six, of Gifford Gardens, exploded before it plunged off the road into Torcido Canyon. Laboratory evidence has uncovered the presence of an explosive device, a bomb, under the cab of the truck. Myers was killed in the explosion and crash. He leaves a wife and two children."

Jaime Salazar stood in dark glasses in glaring sunlight.

"We're talking to Lieutenant Salazar, who is heading up the investigation for the Sheriff's department." The reporter was a chubby-cheeked blond boy. His microphone wore a round red cap to keep the wind out. "Lieutenant, any motive for the killing? The trailer of the truck was empty. Had there been a hijacking?"

"We don't know." The wind blew Salazar's soft, dark hair. He smoothed it with a hand. "It's one of the possibilities we're looking into."

69

"Before we went on the air here," the reporter said, "you mentioned a suspect you wanted to question."

"A convict named Silencio Ruiz," Salazar said.

"Right." The reporter turned to face the camera. "We'll have a photograph of Ruiz on our five o'clock segment of the Channel Three News. Anyone with knowledge of the young man's whereabouts . . ."

"That's your case." Cecil tried not to sound proud.

Dave grunted, frowned, picked up the flimsies, and sorted through them. On the day before he died, Myers had trucked leather coats from a loft in downtown L.A. to a cut-rate retailer in Covina. Later he'd hauled pet supplies from Glendale to Ventura. The manifests had been dropped into the drawer in order, the latest on top, but there was no manifest for what Myers had hauled up Torcido Canyon after midnight. That one would have burned, wouldn't it, with the truck, with the man himself?

"You going to take the shower before I run out of martini?" Cecil watched the tube. He was a news junkie. "In my diminished state, I could dry up and blow away."

"Give me ten minutes." Dave snatched briefs and jeans from an unpainted pine drawer and started down the stairs. "Meantime, phone Jack Schuyler at Pinnacle Life, will you? Introduce yourself and ask him who referred Paul Myers to them. It should be on his application."

The shower didn't take ten minutes. When Dave got back up to the loft, Cecil held out his empty glass. "It was a friend," he said. "Bruce Kilgore."

"Do tell." Dave took the glass, found his own, and made for the cookshack. He hoped a second martini would work up Cecil's appetite. Then they would leave for Max Romano's. Everything on Max's menu was fattening.

9

The van climbed through a crooked pass where ragged rocks thrust up high and cramped the narrow road. And here was the valley. The hills all around were brown, brushy, strewn with bleached boulders. The valley itself was green with groves and meadows. But the sky was hard as he remembered, a relentless Southwest blue, yellow heat in it, even so early in the morning.

Twice Cecil had come out of the back, bored with lying on the couch, watching the coastline, the stucco roadside motels and eateries, the monotonous blue glitter of the Pacific, bored with the magazines he'd brought, the cassettes. Dave had sent him back. Now he came out again and dropped his lanky self into the passenger seat. Dave glanced at him. He looked all right. When he was tired—like last night by the time they'd finished dinner at Max's—his skin took on a dry, dusty finish. It glowed now, and his eyes were clear.

"Pretty," he said. "Picture postcard." He saw something, bent forward, peered upward through the windshield. "Look at that. Hawk circling."

"*Halcón*," Dave said. "That's the name of the place." He saw the hawk and remembered another time when he'd seen a hawk against a sky like this. From the top of a bare, brown mountain back of Sangre de Cristo, up the coast. He'd parked his car outside a bleak concrete-block building there, a television station where a few minutes later he was to encounter Cecil for the first time. He told Cecil about this now. "Maybe it means good luck."

Cecil smiled. "You know it means good luck."

The road sloped down to the valley floor. The tidy rows of round and glossy orange trees looked as if Grant Wood had painted them. Sprinkler pipes worked among the avocado trees, whose branches drooped and tangled. Beneath them the light was undersea light. On tilting, sunswept pastures, Rainbird sprinklers cast sparkling arcs, strewing the grass with emeralds under the hoofs of stocky black cattle that browsed and did not look up as the van passed.

White letters on a modest green sign read HALCON, and here, in the long morning shadows of old live oaks, buildings clustered—metal filling station, railroad-car diner, bat-and-board tavern with COOR's in red neon in the window. The general store was barn-red shiplap, with a long plank front porch and a neat red, white, and blue enamel sign: U.S. POST OFFICE. Dave wheeled the van onto gravel and parked at the end of the long building. He opened the door and stepped stiffly down, glad for the chance to stretch his legs. And a bullet whined past.

Cecil called, "Look out. They're shooting at us."

Dave lay on the ground, the side of his face stung by gravel and by the sharp, dry, curled little leaves of the oaks. Far off, he heard shots. Four, five? He flinched, waiting for the bullets to strike him, to kick up gravel around him, to bore into the sleek metal of the van, to plunk into the crooked gray boles of the oaks. Nothing like that happened. The distant gunfire ceased. Silence. A meadowlark sang.

Nearer, a rooster crowed. Dave turned his head and called:
"Are you all right?"

"I want to go back to the news business," Cecil said.

"Where are you? Your voice sounds funny."

"I am in here with my face in the carpet," Cecil said.
"That can mess up your diction worse than a course in Afro-American English."

"Stay there." Dave rose cautiously. Gravel clung to his face, the heels of his hands. He brushed it off. The van door hung open. He brought his eyes to window level and looked out past the oaks. Flat land stretched away, empty in the sun. Chainlink fencing glinted far off. He wished he had De Witt Gifford's binoculars. Did tiny figures move out there against the dry brown background of the mountains? Was that a line of parked automobiles? Yes. Sunshine glanced off a windowpane. A moment later, dust rose and traveled. A car the size of an ant crawled off. A second. A third. The line of dust stretched out along the foot of the hills. When it settled, he saw no parked cars. He drew a deep breath, straightened, and looked into the van. Cecil had done his panicked best to fit his gangly body under the control panel. Dave reached across and touched him.

"All clear," he said.

Cecil looked up, forehead wrinkled. "Who was it?"

"Too far away to tell," Dave said. "Come on."

Their heels drummed hollowly on the planks of the long porch. Past a screen door, across which angled a shiny metal bar printed DRINK DR. PEPPER, was a wooden door with a top panel of glass. Inside the glass hung a sign: *Closed. Sorry We Missed You, Please Call Again.* Dave read his watch. Two minutes past nine. He went on along the porch with Cecil following. Plank steps went down, and so did they.

Behind the store, a frame cottage stood inside a picket-fenced yard. The house was barn-red, like the store. So was the fence. Grass grew in front of the house. In a bare side yard, white hens pecked near a doghouse that bore the name DIGGER. From a cleat beside the doghouse door a rusty chain hung dragging in the dust. Dave reached over the gate to work the latch, when the house door opened and a stocky brown man came out, buttoning a red and black checkered flannel shirt. His hair was cropped close to his scalp. He pulled the door shut, turned, and gave a little jerk of surprise when he saw Dave and Cecil. He was short, but with a big man's chest and shoulders. He came to the gate bandy-legged in cowboy boots.

"What can I do for you?"

"Tell us about the sharpshooters," Dave said.

The man glanced over his shoulder. "They out there again?"

"Bullet just missed us," Cecil said.

"Damn." It was an apology. "I didn't hear them." He unlatched the gate. "Did they quit at nine?"

"And not a moment too soon," Dave said.

"It's the Sheriff's rifle range." The man let the gate fall shut and walked toward the front of the store. Dave and Cecil followed. Above the beat of their footfalls on the planks, the man said, "Been there forty, fifty years. But I don't think rifles fired so far then." He jingled keys, unlocked the door of the store, and with the scuffed, pointed tip of a boot, kicked a brown rubber wedge under the door to keep it open. "No limit to them now. All the way to Moscow."

The store was gloomy and smelled of onions, cheese, new blue jeans. The man followed a crowded aisle of canned goods—soup, baked beans, chili, Spam—on

74

shelves and in cartons on the floor. He passed out of sight around a stack of new bushel baskets. A cash register beeped. Dodging rakes, hoes, brooms hanging from rafters, Dave and Cecil went after him. He stood behind a counter on whose front a faded sign read KEROSENE. Open boxes of candy bars and chewing gum and digestive tablets lay on the counter. On little wire racks hung cellophane packets of beef jerky, yellow envelopes of corn chips. At his back, shelves held bottles—whiskey, rum, gin, vodka. Cigarette packs were pigeonholed. The man dug a wad of currency from a pocket of his Levi's and sorted the bills into compartments in the shallow gray metal drawer of an electronic cash register. "What I think," he said, "is they want me out of here. Fellow got shot right outside here, four months ago. Walked out with two sacks of steer manure to his car and a bullet hit him. He still don't walk right. They killed my dog."

"Isn't there anything you can do?" Dave said.

"This is the main road," Cecil said. "People could get hit in their cars."

"They have to quit at nine now," the man said. "That was all I could get. County supervisors told them they could only use it in the early morning when there's nobody around. Digger wasn't nobody. Just a dog. They didn't give a damn about a dog." He pushed the cash drawer shut angrily, and the machine emitted a stutter of protesting beeps. "People around here tell me go to court, sue." A wry smile twitched his mouth. "I say, 'I'm no Sioux—I'm a Ute.'" He sobered. "How much do I sue for? Money's not going to get me Digger back. He's dead. Anyway, the lawyers would get all the money. And I haven't got time to hang around courthouses. I got a store to run."

"And a post office," Dave said. From a shirt pocket he

took the slip of paper on which Luther Prentice had written Louella Bishop's address. "Can you tell me how to find this place?" He held out the slip.

The man rummaged under the counter for dime-store reading glasses, put them on, took the slip, peered at it. "Oh, sure." He turned the paper over and, with a ballpoint pen from a plastic cup on the counter, drew a map. "There you go." He handed the paper back to Dave, dropped the pen back into the cup, which had a round, yellow 49¢ EACH sign pasted to it. "Nice lady, Mrs. Bishop. Comes in here a lot. Shops for the Hutchings. Funny thing. You're the second ones to come looking for her." He eyed Cecil. "You a relative?"

Cecil shook his head. "Friend," he said.

Dave said, "Let me tell you who the others were who came looking for her. Last evening, was it?"

"I keep open till nine. Folks forget things, and I'm the only store. They'd have to drive clear up through the pass to town if it wasn't for me."

"A stocky woman," Dave said. "Middle-aged. Well dressed. A pair of big men with her. Goons."

"Drove a white unmarked van," the storekeeper said.

"Right." Dave turned away. "Thank you."

"They called her Duchess," the storekeeper said.

"She wanted to buy the truck." Louella Bishop's haunches were vast as she bent to set breakfast-soiled plates, cups, saucers in the white racks of a dishwasher. Her upper arms were thick as a man's thigh and their flesh jiggled. Above the dishwasher, twin stainless steel sinks were set in a surround of flower-painted shiny Mexican tiles. The electric stove was so surrounded, above it a dark copper-lined hood whose ventilator pipe went up among

76

black rafters. The walls of the kitchen were roughly plastered and very white. The floor was waxed squares of terracotta. In planters outside deep-set windows, geraniums grew intensely green and red in the morning sunshine. Louella Bishop rolled the rack back into place, its glassy burden jingling, and closed the dishwasher door. With a wheeze of breath she straightened up. "And she bought it. Nothing more to tell."

"Why did you sell it?" Dave and Cecil sat at a plank table of wood almost as dark as the rafters, built sometime in the 1920s to imitate a refectory table from a California mission. Coffee mugs were in front of them. "I thought your husband's plan was for Melvil to begin driving as soon as he got out of high school."

"His plan was not to cough and choke himself to death at an early age," Louella Bishop said. "To die in convulsions in the middle of the night. And he gone now. And it's me that going to do the planning now. And it is no way in my plans for Melvil to end up like his father."

"The doctor said it was a heart attack. Dr. Kretschmer. The one who came to your house in Gifford Gardens. The one you called. He didn't put anything about convulsions on the death certificate."

"Ossie—he come home one morning, about three o'clock, three-thirty. He was working nights, you know, to get extra money. They put on all these new taxes—license, tires, no end to it. And he was trying to put money by so as to get another truck, like you say, for Melvil when the time came. We wanted him to get his education first. Anyway"— she filled a mug from a pottery urn, brought it to the table, lowered her bulk onto a chair—"Ossie was sick. Stumbled in the door. Looked like death. Couldn't catch his breath. Says he had to get to the bathroom but he couldn't get across the kitchen. Fell to his hands and knees. Soiled himself, like a little child. Oh, I tell you, that man was sick!" She wagged her head gloomily and sipped her coffee. "Doctor come and give him a shot, and that cleared up the trouble with his bowels."

"Dr. Hobart?" Dave asked.

She looked at him sharply. "Ossie say no Dr. Hobart. Say to call this here Dr. Kretschmer. Something to do with the nightwork. Had to be secret. I shouldn't be telling you, now. I'm talking too much."

"Did the Duchess come with him that time?"

She stirred on the chair, shifting from one mighty flank to the other. She drew a deep breath. Her big bosom rose with it. "I think you better go now."

"What's her real name?" Cecil said.

"Seemed like Ossie was going to get better after that," Louella Bishop said. "But it wasn't more than a few days, and he was dead."

Dave said, "Did Paul Myers come to see your husband when he was sick?"

She frowned. "You say they blew him up?"

"Who do you think they were? The Duchess and her strongarm boys?"

She opened her mouth to answer but she caught herself. "Yes, Paul came. He was a true friend. Had this here magazine with him. Something about science. But I don't know what they talked about. That's the truth. Paul closed the door, and they spoke low. When he left, he was pale, and he was angry." She put her hands flat on the table and heaved herself to her feet. "You best go now. I have a whole big house to clean."

"Why?" Cecil said. "You got a lot of money for that truck. Stands to reason. And what about all the money your husband saved, moonlighting?"

78

"I've got children to raise and send through school. Melvil's going to college. Be something. It's a good place to raise children down here." She rinsed a yellow cellulose sponge at the sink and wiped the handsome tiles. "I worked for the Hutchings before I got married. Says, 'Louella, if ever you want to come back, you come. You a part of this family and you always will be.' And they meant it, too." She glanced at Cecil. "Lord, child, I can't be idle the rest of my days. A person has to work."

Dave rose. "Thank you for your time." He took his coffee mug and Cecil's to the sinks and set them there. "You have no idea who would have wanted to kill Paul Myers? It didn't occur to you that your husband's death wasn't natural? There is no Dr. Kretschmer, you know."

She was wiping the handles of cupboard doors. She frowned at him. "I seen him plain as I see you now."

"He has no address, no telephone number, and no Ford T. Kretschmer is licensed to practice medicine in the state of California." Louella Bishop gave no sign that she was listening. She wiped drawer pulls. Dave said, "The Duchess and her handymen beat up Angela Myers a short time before Paul was killed. These are bad people, Mrs. Bishop. You shouldn't protect them."

"What was your husband hauling for them?" Cecil said.

The massive woman gave him a brief dismissive blink. At the sink she rinsed the sponge again, then took it to the table, bent over the table, began wiping the glossy old planks. She asked Dave, "Did Angela Myers tell you it was them that beat her up?"

"I have a witness. No, she didn't tell me."

"And why not?" Louella Bishop straightened her back and faced Dave, calm, monumental, fists on her hips. "Because she know worse could happen."

Cecil said, "Worse than having her husband killed?"

"She got little children, same as me." Louella Bishop set the chairs neatly at the table. "None of them got any daddy to look out for them now. Nobody but mama." She threw Dave a look of sour reproach. "You think I don't know what kind of people they are?"

"Someone has to stop them," Dave said. "What's her name? She had to sign the check. For the truck."

"Wasn't no check," she said. "She brought cash."

High-school boys in gym trunks collided with each other, dodged and ducked each other, bounced a basketball, threw a basketball, waved their arms, missed the hoop, on sunbaked asphalt beyond a chainlink fence. Their trunks were shiny green. Their skins were shiny with sweat. Up in Los Angeles these days, teenage boys cut their hair short, 1930s-style. Here in the boonies they still wore it long and floppy. Its color ranged from taffy to white, and the skin colors too. But there were two brown-skinned boys and one with black skin.

This was Melvil Bishop. He was thickly built. Basketball wouldn't be his true game, if he had a true game. He looked like a wrestler or a shot putter. He stood by a bench under an old pepper tree and talked to Cecil. Dave watched from the van across the street. Melvil looked sulky. He kept shaking his head. At last, with a bony shrug and a lazy lift of his hand, Cecil came away. He climbed into the cold, conditioned air of the van, looking disgusted.

"Don't help, my being black," he said. "He still would have talked more to you than he did to me. He never saw the Duchess before last night, never saw the phony doctor, never saw the heavies. His father died of a heart attack. He never said what he was hauling in his truck at night, or who he was working for. The old preacher is lying; Melvil never said anything to his mother about any doctor at any grave. Louella Bishop is just plain scared. Melvil—I'd say he was scared with all the extras."

"You want to drive now?" Dave said.

Cecil brightened. "All the way home?"

"Till you get tired," Dave said.

They changed seats and Cecil started the engine. "Why did the Duchess buy that truck?" He released the parking brake, frowned into the side mirror, steered the van down the sleepy morning street past old white frame cottages. A dog ran out and raced beside them, barking and trying to nip the tires. "Jesus." Cecil twisted the steering wheel, left, right. The tires squealed. "That is one ignorant dog. Going to get himself killed." Sweat broke out on Cecil's forehead. He pawed for the buttons that controlled the windows. His window slid down. "Get away, fool. Get away." He tramped on the brakes.

"Take it easy," Dave said. "He'll be all right."

It was the end of the dog's block. He left off barking and chasing, trotted back across the street, and went uphill along a sidewalk strewn with bright children's toys, his plumy tail waving. Cecil leaned his head on the steering wheel. He was trembling. "Shit," he said. He sat up and for a moment stared straight ahead through the windshield. He shivered. Eyes shut, he drew in air deeply, held it, blew it out. It didn't stop his trembling. Dave touched him. He looked at Dave. Tears were in his eyes. "I can't do it. Can't even drive a car anymore."

"You can," Dave said. "Of course you can. Just get your composure back, now. It's all right. Everything's cool. The dog is fine. No harm done."

But Cecil shook his head and lifted his butt up off the dark blue velvet of the driver's seat. Dave swiveled aside, then slid back of him and sat behind the wheel. Cecil sat in the passenger seat, long fingers interlaced hard between his knees. He sat looking down at his hands and said nothing. Dave got the van to Main Street, with its sallow brick and bright signs and dusty pickup trucks and shiny shopping carts. He got the van out of town, brown hills on the right, blue glitter of ocean on the left. He looked at Cecil. His eyes were closed again. Tears ran down his face. Tissues were in a dark blue box on the control panel. Dave pulled two out and nudged Cecil with the hand that held the tissues. Cecil opened his eyes, mutely accepted the tissues, wiped his face, dropped the wet tissues into the blue trash receptacle, clasped his hands between his knees again, slumped in the seat, chin on his chest.

"We can stop for a drink," Dave said. "Will that help?"

Cecil said, "You don't understand, do you?"

"I'd like to," Dave said. "Why don't you make me?"

Cecil managed a damp, crooked smile. "I'll make you later. Now, I'll explain." He looked somber. "You know what is going to happen to me if a bullet ever comes at me again? I am going to die. I don't mean if it hits me. If it hits me or not, I am going to die. Rifle range? Shit!"

"You held up fine all morning," Dave said.

"What kind of dog do you think Digger was? 'They killed my dog,' the man said." Cecil swiveled the seat, stared straight ahead again, fingers of both hands pressed flat against his mouth, tears running again. At last he dropped his hands. He drew a long, shuddering breath. "When he said that, I could feel the bullet going in. I don't want to kill anybody's dog."

"Right," Dave said, and handed him more tissues.

Cecil dried his eyes and blew his nose. He dropped the used tissues into the blue bin. "Why did the Duchess buy

82

that truck?" he said. "Why now? Why not before? This a long way to come."

"Since she got here before nine," Dave said, "she must have left L.A. about the time of the afternoon news. When they said the Sheriff didn't think it was an accident anymore, what happened to Paul Myers."

"So what happened to Ossie Bishop wasn't an accident, either? And the truck has got evidence in it of that?"

Dave smiled. "You have a future in this business."

"If I can keep away from bullets," Cecil said. "If I can keep away from dogs."

10

Dave swung the van in at the Myers driveway, those two narrow strips of cracked cement leading past the side of the house to the garage, whose overhead door gaped, slumping in the middle. Dave slid the van into the garage and stopped it. "Come on," he said. "On the double." He jumped down out of the van and so did Cecil. Outside, Dave reached and caught a frayed rope end and dragged the garage door down. "If nobody's watching, it will be safe for a few minutes."

Cecil glanced around. "I don't like the odds."

"We're not staying." Dave crossed grass so dry it crackled underfoot. At the back door, he rapped the frame of the screen with his knuckles. No one stirred inside the house. He peered, holding hands at his eyes as blinkers. The sun was far to the west and low, but it still glared against the smoggy sky. He could make out nothing indoors. Cecil climbed on a bricked square meant for a planter, in which nothing grew but a few dry weeds. He peered through a window. "Looks like nobody's home," he said.

"That's all right. I didn't come to talk to anyone." Dave slipped a thin steel pick from his wallet and worked the screen-door lock. The lock of the wooden door, with its glass pane, was even easier. That required only the insertion of a credit card between lock and frame. When the door opened, the children's artwork fastened to the refrigerator fluttered. Empty beer cans stood on the kitchen table, a full ashtray. Dirty dishes were piled in the sink. The smell this time was of peanut butter. Dave left the kitchen for the hall.

The door to the children's room was open. Inside, a portable radio whispered rock music. Nothing in Angela Myers's bedroom was different from before except that possibly more underclothes were strewn around. Dave went straight to the closet, straight to the drawer with the shipping manifests. He knelt, pulled it open, and released breath he hadn't even known he was holding. He'd feared Salazar might have beaten him to it. Or the Duchess. This time he took them all. Half the stack he handed up to Cecil.

"Stash those on you, out of sight," he said. The other half he folded and pushed into the inner pocket of his jacket. He closed the drawer and rose. "Let's go."

They were rolling backward out the narrow driveway when someone shouted. Dave braked the van. Weighed down by bulging white plastic supermarket sacks, Gene Molloy halted on the front sidewalk. The children were with him. Each of them carried a sack. Molloy set his down and jogged to the van. "I want to talk to you," he said. "I want to show you something. Better not leave this out where the jigs can see it." He meant the van. In the sun glare he hadn't noticed Cecil. Or maybe he had and didn't care. "Put it in the garage and close the door," he said. "I'll let you in the back way." He let them in the back way, frowning. "I know damn well I locked these doors."

"This is my associate, Cecil Harris," Dave said. "Gene

Molloy." Molloy shook Cecil's hand, but his Irish eyes were not smiling. Cecil muttered something polite. Dave said, "Did you ever hear your brother-in-law mention someone called the Duchess?"

Brian, the Myers boy with the white sheepdog hair, took cans out of the slithery white sacks that lay bulging on the kitchen chairs. He climbed a short aluminum ladder to stow the cans on cupboard shelves. He set boxes—cereal, crackers, tea bags—on the shelves. Stretching, he put plastic-wrapped chicken legs and hamburger into the freezer. A deep tin drawer rattled when he opened it to drop in lettuce, tomatoes. carrots.

"I told you," Molloy said, "I wasn't around here that much. A Duchess? What kind of sense does that make?"

"A nickname. Someone he worked for. Possibly the one he was working for nights."

Cecil helped the child by arranging boxes of frozen vegetables along a freezer-door shelf. He said, "Possibly the one who killed him."

Molloy glared at him. "Watch your mouth."

Cecil touched the boy's shoulder. "I'm sorry."

"It's not your fault," the boy said. He looked at Molloy. "I did my half. It's Ruth Ann's turn."

"Go get her," Molloy said. And to Dave, "It wasn't any Duchess. I know who it was. I've got proof. Come on. I'll show you." He left the kitchen for the living room. Up the hall, the rock music was loud now. And louder still were the voices of Brian and Ruth Ann. Quarreling. Molloy turned back, pushed past Dave and Cecil, went to the door of the children's bedroom, and put his head inside. "Knock it off. Right now. Ruth Ann, God damn it." He disappeared into the room. The music broke off. "Get out to that kitchen and put the rest of those groceries away, and when you finish with that, wash the dishes. By yourself."

"See, stupid," Brian's voice said.

"I'll stupid you," Ruth Ann's voice said.

She came out of the room with Molloy behind her, his hands on her shoulders. When he had deposited her in the kitchen he came into the living room, where Dave and Cecil stood waiting. "Look at these," he said, and dug under the cushions of the sofa and brought out crumpled sheets of paper. He pushed them at Dave, who took them, frowned, reached for his reading glasses, turned the pages around, studied them. Cecil peered over his shoulder. Molloy lit a cigarette and smiled grimly. "You know what those are?"

"This is Kilgore School stationery," Dave said. "Is this Brian's work, Ruth Ann's? They look like diagrams."

"I don't think any kids drew those," Cecil said.

"I'm ashamed to have to say it," Molloy said, "but Bruce Kilgore has been sleeping with my sister."

"So I've heard," Dave said.

"What do you think his reason was?" A crash sounded from the kitchen. Molloy grimaced and left the room. Ruth Ann wailed. Molloy shouted. Dave frowned at the copies of *Scientific American* on the coffee table. He picked up the top one and leafed through it. Silence reigned in the kitchen. Molloy returned with cans of beer. He handed one to Dave, one to Cecil, and popped the opener tab on one for himself. "Maybe you think it was love," he said.

"Possibly loneliness," Dave said. He held up the magazine. "I'd like to borrow this, if I may."

Molloy shrugged. "Be my guest. I can't read the God damn things. No, there's lots of lonely housewives. Why Angie? She's sure as hell no *Playboy* centerfold."

"What are you trying to say?" Dave rattled the papers. "What have these got to do with it?"

"Look." Molloy sat on the couch and balanced his beer

can on the arm. A large, thick book lay on the coffee table with the magazines. Molloy sat forward, spread the book open, leafed over glossy pages, some of them smeared and thumb-printed. It was a truck-repair manual. When Molloy found the page he wanted, he slapped it and reached up for the Kilgore School papers. Dave handed them to him. Molloy swiveled the book so it faced Dave, and laid the pages beside it. "Check this out."

Dave bent above the book, hands on knees, the glasses slipping down his nose. The diagram in the book covered two pages. It detailed the air-brake system of an eighteen-wheel truck and trailer. The Kilgore School pages broke the diagram into three parts, but each part had plainly been copied from this book or another book of the same sort. Dave pushed the glasses up his nose, and straightened. He said, "You think Bruce Kilgore drew these?"

"I found them in the dumpster back of the school. I knew what they were right away. When Paul did let me live here, he made me help him do maintenance on the truck. I don't think Kilgore ever did maintenance on a truck. He had to copy the diagram because he doesn't know it by heart the way any trucker would."

Cecil tilted his head. "You think Kilgore wanted to kill your brother-in-law by rigging the brakes on his truck? But that wasn't how it happened."

"It was just his first idea," Molloy said. "I don't know why he changed his mind. But he could make a bomb easy. He's a trained engineer."

"What would be the point?" Dave took off the glasses, folded them, pushed them away. "To marry your sister, and use the insurance money to bail out his school?"

Molloy frowned. "You been thinking that too?"

"What does Salazar think?" Dave said.

Molloy laid the pages in the big book and shut it with a thud. Mouth a tight line, he twisted out his cigarette in the fluted pink china ashtray. "He hasn't got time to see me." Molloy slumped back on the couch, gulped beer. "That's why I'm glad you showed up today. He's your buddy. If you tell him about Kilgore, maybe he'll tear himself away from that moron street-gang shootup for five minutes."

"Where was that? When?"

"Yesterday. Sundown." Molloy fingered another cigarette from the pocket of his sweaty T-shirt, faded red with STUD POWER lettered across the chest. "Silencio Ruiz and his hot tamales." Molloy scratched a paper match and lit the cigarette. "Raided a barbecue at the nig—" He darted a glance at Cecil and changed the word. "At the black church on Guava Street. Mount Olivet? Free food, so guess what? The Edge showed up to eat it, didn't they? You should have seen it." He waved his beer can at the gray-faced portable television by the couch. "Blood and barbecue sauce all over the place."

"We'd better go." Dave set his beer can on the table. It was still full. Cecil set his beside it and followed Dave, who took long strides toward the kitchen. Molloy jumped up. "You tell Salazar for me, okay? About Kilgore? All he can think about now is Ruiz."

Dave stopped in the doorway from hall to kitchen. "Did they catch him? Is he locked up?"

"It happened too fast. They came through those walnut trees screaming and shooting and in a minute, ninety seconds, it was all over. They were gone. They rounded up most of them later. But not Silencio. He got away."

Ruth Ann stood on the aluminum ladder stool and fitted a roll of paper towels on a rack beside the window over the kitchen sink. The dishes in the sink floated in sudsy water.

So did the plastic wrapper from the paper towels. Dave and Cecil went to the outside kitchen door.

"Goodbye," Ruth Ann said.

"Wait a second," Molloy said. He held the edge of the wooden door. "Did Mr. Smithers contact you?"

"I've been out of town," Dave said. "Who is Smithers?"

"Oh, shit," Molloy said. "You don't know him? He was here last night, suppertime. Said it was about Paul's insurance. Wanted to talk to Angie. Asked the same questions you did. I told him you'd already been here. He said it was a communications mixup, and apologized and left. Tall guy, thin, bald." Molloy studied Dave. "Must be big bucks in checking insurance claims. He drove a Mercedes."

"Did it leave here on its wheels?" Cecil said.

"The gangs were busy at the church," Molloy said.

Dave said, "Have you got Smithers's card?"

"He didn't give me one. I showed him yours. I think he put it in his pocket. What's it all about?"

Dave tugged at the doorknob. Molloy let the door go. Dave swung it open, pushed the screen door, stepped out and down. "I'll tell you when I have a chance to look into it. It's probably as he says." Dave watched Cecil lope to the garage and raise the warped door. "Just a mixup. I was hired from outside. He's probably from inside." Dave lifted a hand, started to turn away.

"Maybe." Molloy stood holding the screen door open, beer can in his hand. "But there's one funny thing. Angie told me. Smithers went to the restaurant, Cappuccino's, right? Where she works? He ordered dinner, but he didn't eat it. All he did was ask her questions."

11

He stopped the van behind the cinder-block church through whose thin yellow paint the shadowy street-gang *placa* showed. An old gray Ford LTD sedan waited back here. It was beautifully kept, not a dent in it, the paint glossy as new. Dave switched off the engine of the van and sat for a moment beside Cecil, looking at the walnut grove. Under the trees, the long picnic tables lay on their sides. Steel folding chairs had been overturned. Among the branches, lights had been strung. Many of the sockets showed splintered stumps of bulb. One string had come down and trailed on the ground among paper plates and plastic utensils that glinted in the dying daylight. Raw wood shone through the torn bark of trees, pale white. The leaves of trees hung tattered. Round green walnut husks strewed the ground.

"Machine guns?" Cecil said.

"God knows." Dave climbed down from the van. In the evening hush, music came from the church—piano, voices. Cecil stood listening. Dave pressed the bell push beside the rectory door, over the weathered business card of Luther Prentice, D.D. But it was Mrs. Prentice who came to the door. She didn't look so tall now. Maybe it was the black dress. She looked old and weary. "I came," Dave said, "to tell you that I'm shocked and sorry this happened. Can I help in any way?" He glanced toward the trees. "I might have been here, you know. Reverend Prentice invited me."

She made a grim sound. "It's as well you weren't."

Still standing beside the van, his face turned toward the music, Cecil sang softly to himself, "'Amazing grace, how—'"

"They are rehearsing," Mrs. Prentice said, and came out to stand on the step. "For the funeral. It will be a communal funeral. Five dead, you know. One minute eating, laughing, having a fine time. Next minute, dead on the ground in their own blood."

"The boys from The Edge?"

A bitter smile moved her mouth. "It was supposed to be them. That was what they came for. But it was only two of them got hit at all." She looked quickly at Dave. "I mean that's terrible enough. But they will be all right. The ones who died—they were just in the way."

"That's where your husband is?" Dave said. "With the families?"

She nodded. "A mother dead, not thirty years old, three little children left behind. A boy fourteen, could play any instrument you put in his hands. A wonderful, talented boy with such a marvelous future ahead of him in this world. We need all the beauty we can get, it seems to me." A black handbag was in her hand. She dug in it for a handkerchief and touched her wet eyes. "I know I wasn't meant to understand Our Father, but sometimes I wish He would let me understand. An old man going, like Mr. Jackson, that's not so hard. But that fine young boy, and the others in the sunshine of their days. We needed them here."

"What was the reason for the raid?" Dave said.

"Reason?" Her laugh was bleak. "The Edge boys were bound to be here, weren't they, and they wouldn't be expecting a fight, wouldn't be ready for it. Hatred's the only reason I can give you. But it seems as though hatred is enough." She looked at the watch on her thin wrist. "You must excuse me now. I have a good many visits to make at the hospital." She pulled the house door shut. Her eyes begged Dave for an answer. "Where did they get guns like that, that fire so fast, so many bullets it seemed like rain?"

"Guns are big business these days," Dave said. "Did you see Silencio Ruiz? Do you know him when you see him?"

"Oh, yes." She stepped past Dave and unlocked the gray car. "They are saying on the news that he led the raid." She bent to get into the car, then straightened and rolled down the window of the open door. "They are saying no such things happened while he was away in prison." She took the handkerchief from her bag again, and stooped a little, and waved the handkerchief inside the car, as if to stir the air that had baked itself in there. "They are saying he must have got them the guns—something he learned in prison."

Dave stared. "And you don't think so?"

"He was trying to stop them" She got into the car, behind the steering wheel, and stretched across to roll down the window on the passenger side. Sweat broke out on her face, and she wiped it with the handkerchief. "Car gets so hot. I don't remember when we ever had weather like this."

Dave frowned down at her, his hands on the window ledge of the car door. "Why would he try to stop them? He was their leader."

"Used to be, I know." She dug keys from the handbag in her lap, set the handbag beside her on the seat, fitted the key into the ignition lock. "But, you see, he didn't come with them." She turned the key. The engine started. It ran so quietly it sounded new. She looked up at Dave. "He came from the street. He ran in amongst the tables. Now I don't understand but a little bit of Spanish, but the way he was waving his arms at them and shouting and the expression on his face—it was plain to me he wanted them to stop. Wonder is he wasn't killed himself."

"Did you report this to Lieutenant Salazar?"

She managed a wan smile. "He said I was mistaken." The parking brake made a clunk when she released it with her foot. Her hand came out to take the inside door latch. Dave let go of the door and stepped back. "I was not mistaken. I was here. And I know what I saw." She pulled the door shut. "I was right there, at the corner of the house, with a fresh platter of barbecued wings. I wasn't in the line of fire. I didn't have to crouch down under the tables like the rest. I saw. I saw it all. And he was trying to stop them." She gave her head a sorry shake. "But it seems I was the only one who did, and one old black woman's word is not enough." She glanced at her watch again. "Oh, dear. I am very late. I must go. Excuse me."

"Just one more minute." Dave put on his glasses, drew a leather folder from his jacket, leaned on the hot hood of the car, and wrote a check. He tore it from the pad and handed it to her. She blinked in surprise. Putting away the folder, he said, "I've made it out to the church. You see that whoever needs it gets it, all right?"

She read the check and her eyes widened. "But this is a great deal of money." She stared at him, openmouthed.

He smiled. "Money isn't what it used to be."

She laughed. "Truly. When I was a little girl in Georgia, my whole family could have lived for a year on this." She

94

folded the check and tucked it into her purse. She looked at him solemnly. "Bless you," she said.

Cecil said, "Excuse me, but the Edge boys, the wounded ones, will they be in that hospital too?"

"Mrs. Prentice," Dave said, "this is my associate, Cecil Harris."

She nodded. "Yes. And if it's like last night and this morning, the others will be there too, the ones that weren't hurt, and some that didn't come to the picnic at all. They'll be in the rooms, in the halls, guarding their friends, seeing that nothing more happen to them. The authorities don't like it, but they're afraid to order them out."

"Oh, yes, I saw it." De Witt Gifford had painted his face. Rouge was thick on the wrinkled cheekbones above his beard. In the murky light of the attic it looked black. So did the slash of red that was his mouth. He had shaved off his eyebrows and drawn them thin and high and arched. Blue paint was above his curious eyes. Out in the daylight, he had looked like the bearded lady left behind by some circus that had pulled up stakes and departed town fifty years ago. His hat, this time, was a high-crowned blue-black straw, entangled in netting. He pulled it off and tossed it on the bed as his motor-chair whined past. Its wheels bumped him into the tower. "From here there's quite a good view. Of course, the walnut trees interfered. I couldn't see it all. But I saw enough. It was horrible."

"It was the gang you sponsored," Dave said. "You bought them those green jackets."

"Don't throw my follies up to me," Gifford said. "I can't change the past. Good God. The only philanthropic gesture in my selfish life, and look what it gets me." He picked the big binoculars up off the windowsill and peered through them out the clean, curved glass. "Obloquy. Well, I assure you, I am not to blame for that raid. I am sickened by it. Absolutely revolted."

"The jackets weren't your only philanthropic gesture," Dave said. "There was another. You bailed Silencio Ruiz out of jail after his arrest for holding up that supermarket. You hired a high-priced defense attorney for him."

Gifford sat motionless in slim, ragged silhouette against the dying light of the hot day. He seemed not to breathe. Then he breathed, but he did not turn. "No wonder you can afford the clothes you wear and the cars you drive. You are very good at your work. Did they tell you these things downtown? Or was it Bruce Kilgore?"

"He figures his vow of silence isn't sacred anymore. In his estimation, you didn't keep your end of the bargain. You see, he thinks Silencio blew up Paul Myers's truck. And he's not alone. The Sheriff thinks so too."

Gifford set the binoculars down and turned. The backlight of the windows made a scarecrow halo of his white hair and beard. "And you? I really don't give a hoot what Kilgore thinks. He's a clod. The police are"—he shrugged bony shoulders under a moth-eaten afghan—"we all know what the police are. What do *you* think? That I would find interesting."

Dave smiled. "I think I'd like a drink. You?"

Gifford's laugh was a crackle of dead leaves. "Of course. When wouldn't I? You know where the bottles are, I believe?"

Dave switched on lights in the tidy kitchen. Two plates drained in the rubber rack beside the small sink. Two forks lay there also, and two spoons. Two blue pottery bowls drained upside down. In the sink, with water standing in them, were aluminum-foil trays that had held, at a guess, frozen enchiladas. The water was chili red. Dave found glasses, ice cubes, Scotch, switched off the light, returned to the tower with the drinks. He put one in Gifford's claw, and with his own drink sat on the Empire couch with its threadbare Spanish shawl. The cushioning of the couch made dry sounds under him like very brittle straw.

"Lieutenant Salazar reasons this way," he said. "No sooner is Silencio out of prison than Paul Myers is murdered. And where is Silencio? Nobody knows. He sees his parents only once, fails to report to his parole officer, sees nothing of his gang. He vanishes. That is suspicious."

"Thank you for the drink." Gifford held it to his mouth and sipped from it, small sips, one every few seconds. He was gazing out the window. "It was not quite, I think, the most shocking thing I ever saw. No, it wouldn't be, would it? Nothing can shock us as things do in childhood. I told you how I used to creep down by the creek at night. Interesting things went on down there under the oaks and in the brush close to the water. I remember it had rained for days. Then the storm passed and we had a glorious day. That night, the stars were bright, the moon was very full. It shone on me and woke me, and I crept out. The house was asleep. The ground, of course, was still wet. So I thought no one would be out there, making love as they liked to do. There'd be nothing interesting to watch. Nothing educational.

"But there was. A young woman—a girl, really, as I see her now—probably fifteen, sixteen. I was perhaps ten or eleven. And something seemed to be wrong with her. I was vastly ignorant. She was all alone, half hidden in the undergrowth, writhing on the ground, moaning, whimpering to herself. In Spanish. Prayers. I won't go on with the details. She was giving birth. I can't tell you how dumbfounded I was when this wet, struggling thing came from her in the moonlight. The scream she gave is still in my ears. I understood and didn't understand. I turned my face away. I'm afraid I threw up.

"And when I looked again, she was on her feet, clutching the baby. It was gasping, crying. Like a sick cat. And she ran down to the creek with it. And without a sound, without a moment's pause, she threw it into the rushing water. I heard a scream and looked around to see who it was, but of course it was me, wasn't it? It frightened the girl. She ran away, slipping, sliding, falling.

"I rushed down to the creek, stumbled in up to my waist. The current was very strong. I wanted to save the baby. I couldn't see it. I called and called. As if a newborn child would know it was being called to. I knelt in the rocks and splashed around for it with my hands. But I didn't find it. It was gone. The creek had it."

"Sounds like a dream," Dave said. "You sure it wasn't a dream?"

"I hoped so, next morning. But my clothes were still wet. And they found the baby. Miles downstream. The story was in the newspaper. I clipped it out and kept it. I suppose I still have it somewhere. They never found the girl. My God, she's an old woman by now. Or dead. At my time of life, you look around, and everyone you ever knew is dead. My glass is empty."

Dave rose and took the glass. "Silencio's gang killed five people. Not one of them was a member of The Edge."

"It's not Silencio's gang," Gifford said sharply.

"He was there. The minister's wife says so. You saw it too. Wasn't he there?"

"If I were Silencio," Gifford said, "I should be hiding somewhere. He must know they believe he killed Paul

Myers. He's such an obvious suspect. He'd be a fool to add to his troubles by leading that raid."

"Mrs. Prentice says he was trying to stop it. The Sheriff won't believe her. She needs a backup. Silencio needs a backup. You sure you didn't see what she saw?"

"I told you." Gifford motioned at the window. "The tree-tops. I only got glimpses. But Silencio didn't lead that raid. He was through with gangs. Prison cured him of that. He came to see me, briefly, the day he returned from San Quentin. He told me, and I believed him. Now could I have my drink?"

Dave fetched it. "Last night at six, a tall, bald man in a Mercedes stopped at Myers's. You notice fine cars. Did you see it? Did you happen to get the license number?"

Gifford drank from his glass. "I was watching the church, the walnut grove."

Going out through the shadows of the garret, Dave jerked his head aside to avoid the pale canvas corner of the old life raft. The elevator creaked him down to the deserted pantry. He stood frowning while the elevator door slid shut. He listened. No dogs whined or snuffled behind closed doors. The looming old house stood hollow, silent, empty of life. He walked out into the hallway beside the great, gloomy staircase, thinking his footfalls might rouse the dogs. No such thing.

He opened doors and peered into shrouded rooms that breathed dust, mildew, neglect at him. He went back the way he had come and into the gaunt, disused kitchen. It smelled of dogs. He crossed scuffed linoleum, pulled open a door, and found himself on a screened porch where an old oaken icebox lurked, and an old Maytag washer with gray, crumbling wringers. A strong latch was on the screen door. A pair of bolts of bright new metal. But not fastened. He pushed the door open. Wooden steps, frail with age, went down to what must once have been the kitchen garden Gifford had mentioned—where there was always fresh mint. It was weeds and creepers now, matted, brittle.

Beyond it, a hurricane fence crossed, barbwire-topped. And a few yards farther off, an old stable building reared up, jigsaw work along its eaves, slats broken out of its cupola. The stable door stood open. The glare of the setting sun was in Dave's eyes, but he thought he saw movement inside the stable. He waited, squinting, straining his ears. But the building was too far off. He started to take a step down, then thought better of it. It looked to him as if the gate in the fence was ajar. The stable and the yard were probably where the dogs stayed when not on duty. He didn't want to meet the dogs. He stepped back onto the porch and was just letting the screen door fall shut when he heard a dog bark.

A man yelped, "Lady, no! Damn it, come back here."

Out the stable door, dragging a large, heavy, green paper sack, came a big, lean Doberman. The man appeared. He was slender, brown-skinned, curly-haired. He lunged for the sack, grabbed it, tugged, and the sack split open. Kibbled dog food rattled on the hard ground. The young man took a laughing swing at the dog, who dodged away. The young man hung for a moment on hands and knees, wagging his head in amused despair over the spilled food, the torn sack—then jumped to his feet and went back into the stable. He spoke the dog's name, but she didn't respond. She stood at the fence, staring through at Dave.

Dave let the porch door close softly and went back through the dark house and let himself out through the front doors, with their etched-glass panels.

It wasn't far to the hospital, but by the time he reached

it, all light had gone from the sky. He left the van in the parking lot slot of some doctor he hoped had gone home for the day or wouldn't arrive too soon. The parking lot was otherwise filled, unbroken rows of cars—a number of them Mustangs in various stages of repair—among the long strips of ivy geranium and the decorative palms. The long, curved fronds of the palms blew in a southeast wind that had risen with the coming of night. The wind was cool and Dave turned up his jacket collar, making his way toward the lighted glass side doors of the hospital. He looked up bleakly at the ten stories of shining windows, and lowered his eyes. He didn't want to think about the misery behind the glass. His horror of hospitals had been sharpened by Cecil's recent ordeal. But it had originated when Rod Fleming died slowly in a hospital a dozen years ago—of a kind of cancer they were now learning how to cure. There was no humor in the irony of that. He had lived with Rod for twenty-two years. He would never stop missing him.

But his spirits lightened when he found Cecil in a big, lamplit room of couches and easy chairs, where the sick and the well made ready to leave this place. Cecil sat talking with Luther Prentice, whose glasses and bald head gleamed. Cecil saw Dave coming, making his way through a clutter of empty wheelchairs, and smiled and waved. Dave smiled back. He shook Prentice's long, kindly hand. The preacher said, "My wife tells me you have made a generous donation to the victims of the shooting. Please accept my gratitude. It was a terrible thing to happen. I don't know what I was thinking of, bringing all those people there, putting them in danger of their lives." Behind the shiny lenses, his eyes misted. "I have asked the Lord to forgive me for my foolishness, and I expect He has, but I don't know that I will ever be able to forgive myself."

"You only wanted to feed people," Cecil said.

"You couldn't know what would happen," Dave said.

"Someone more worldly-wise than I am"—Prentice shook his head sorrowfully—"would have realized that with their leader back out of prison, that gang would get up to something evil again."

"Your wife doesn't think it was Silencio's doing," Dave said. "She thinks he was trying to stop it."

Prentice's smile was gently tolerant. "She is even less worldly-wise than I am." He sighed. "No, I'm afraid this is only the beginning of the shootings, ambushes, deaths. The Edge will want revenge. And then—" He straightened. "Ah, here comes Mrs. Prentice now." He looked at an old silver watch on a bony wrist. "She is behind time. Prayer meeting begins at seven."

She came and spoke in her soft, musical voice to Dave and Cecil, her gentle brown eyes reflecting the suffering she had just been witness to, even while she smiled politely at these two strangers. Then she and her stilt-tall husband excused themselves and went away into the night. Luther Prentice's voice drifted back as he pushed open the heavy glass door for her. "We'll be late."

"The Lord will wait," she said. "He always has."

Dave said to Cecil, "Is he right? Are there going to be more ambushes, more deaths?"

"It's a good thing all the G-G's are in jail," Cecil said. "If The Edge ever gets hold of any of them, they won't live through it."

"Shall we go?" Dave said, and moved back toward the wheelchairs, toward the parking-lot doors beyond the wheelchairs. Cecil came along behind.

He said, "I'll be glad to get out of here. I've had enough of hospitals to last me the rest of my life." Dave pushed the door open. Wind gusted in. "Whoo! That is cold." The door closed behind them. Cecil put his head down and hugged himself. They trotted toward the van. "Spooky wind, too. Can't make up its mind where it's coming from." They climbed into the van and slammed the doors. "Hot today, too." Cecil shivered and rubbed his arms.

"Looks like the end of summer," Dave said. He started the engine. "You talked to The Edge. Which ones?"

"Rollo Poore. He's the head honcho. He's got a bullet in his thigh. Must have been some bullet. I would judge him to be made of some very tough alloy. I tried to talk to the ones leaning around looking mean in the hallways, but Rollo—he the spokesman. Nobody else gave me squat. All they did was point at this particular room and say, 'Talk to Rollo Poore.'"

Dave backed the van, changed gears, joined the red and yellow lights of traffic heading away from Gifford Gardens toward the freeway. "And what did Rollo say?"

"You should have seen that room. Like something out of an old Edward G. Robinson movie, only all black, of course. The heavy standing outside the door. The heavy leaning against the wall by the window. Sulky. Watching me like he was thinking up ways to take me apart and put me back together again all wrong. Mrs. Prentice—I saw her before I saw Rollo. She said the authorities won't let The Edge carry weapons. No weapons in the hospital, she said. But I swear, the one in the room had a gun stuck in his pants. His jacket covered it, but it was there."

"I'm sorry," Dave said. "I ought to have gone."

"You're the wrong color. He'd never have talked to you." Cecil had stopped shivering. "It's a good heating system in this van. Rollo said, when he gets out of bed, he and the rest of them are going to find Silencio Ruiz and kill him. How was your crazy old peeper today?"

"Makeup an inch thick," Dave said. "He denied it before, but he has a man around the house. I wondered who smoked the cigarettes, who washed the windows, kept the kitchen and the bathroom spic and span. I wondered who looked after the dogs. I saw him today."

"Hired hand?" Cecil asked.

"They take their meals together," Dave said. "I don't know what else they do together. What does Silencio Ruiz look like? Did you see his picture on the news last night? Well built, six feet, curly hair? Ramon Novarro?"

"I don't know who that might be," Cecil said, "but if you mean is he pretty, you got it."

"He was feeding the dogs," Dave said. "It figures. Gifford's been looking out for him for a long time."

"That was why he paid off Bruce Kilgore not to leak it about the bail and the expensive lawyer. To keep Silencio's gang from suspecting what was between him and Gifford. It wouldn't fit the macho image."

"That's the explanation that makes sense," Dave said.

"And when Silencio learned about Paul Myers's death, he ran to Gifford's enchanted castle to hide out, right? Lucky old Gifford." They sloped onto the freeway. "What are you going to do?"

"Tell Salazar." Rain began to spatter the windshield. "Get Silencio into jail with the rest of the G-G's. To keep The Edge from killing him." Dave switched on the wipers. "And that silly old man."

12

I t was a lazy rain, the warm, tropical sort that now and then drifts up from Mexico. It fell all night on the shingles above the loft and made sleeping good. It was still coming down from ragged, gray-black clouds when they went their separate ways next morning. Cecil took his van. Dave took the sideswiped car. Rain had leaked into it, probably because the rubber around the doors was rotten. The floor was puddled. The rubber of the wiper blades was also shot. He stopped at a filling station for new ones, then wheeled onto the first of three freeways that would take him out east of Pasadena to a plant called Tech-Rite. That name, and the names Chemiseal and Agroplex on the new batch of waybills taken from Paul Myers's closet drawer, had interested Dave.

Tech-Rite occupied long buildings far off across empty land backed by rain-shrouded mountains. The buildings were flat-roofed, windowless, featureless. Big white storage tanks loomed behind them. To a security guard in a black rubber hat and poncho, Dave showed his license and explained his business. The guard made a phone call from inside his white stucco booth. Light flickered off his rain-slick poncho from a small black-and-white television set in the booth. He hung up the phone and came down out of the booth and leaned to the car window. A gnarled hand pushed something shiny at Dave, a card enfolded in clear plastic, printed with the name TECH-RITE, the word VISITOR, and some blank lines.

"Write your name on there, will you?" the guard said. "Truth is, I'm supposed to, but I can't hold a pen too good anymore." He appeared past retirement age. The raindrops on his drooping, hound-dog face looked like tears. "When your name is on it, pin it to your jacket and I'll open the gates and you can drive on in."

Dave did as he was told. The guard continued to lean at the window, watching but probably not seeing. Dave pricked a finger pushing the pin through his lapel. He sucked the finger. "That do it?"

"Fine, thanks." The guard stepped creakily up into the booth again and shut the door. The wide, high, chainlink gates swung open. Dave drove the rattly car through, and headed it up a two-lane strip of blacktop that glistened in the rain. He passed parking lots filled with cars parked on the bias in neat, shiny rows. He drove on. A sign read EXECUTIVE PARKING LOT. He slowed and almost swung in at the arrow painted on the paving, then saw ahead through the rain another sign—VISITORS. He left the battered Valiant there, among new Audis, Cutlasses, BMWs, and hurried, head down, toward double glass doors that glowed with light in the bleak, unbroken plane of the building front.

He waited an hour for Lorin Shields, in the reception room of offices marked PUBLIC RELATIONS. He was not neglected. He was served tea from a Worcester pot in a Worcester cup and saucer. At a guess, English breakfast tea. There were English muffins. There was English marmalade. The young woman who served them on a Japanese lacquer tray was oriental herself. She apologized smoothly and smilingly for Shields's tardiness at first. He was rarely late. It must be the rain. He had a long way to come. But as time dragged on, she became embarrassed. Little lines appeared between her beautiful brows when she glanced up from the whispering electronic typewriter at her desk, saw Dave, saw the clock.

Dave, trying to make sense of a trade journal article on the molecular structure of a new breed of plastics, gave her a smile. "It's all right. I have no other appointments. I don't mind waiting."

"I can't think why he hasn't telephoned."

In the end, a blond, rosy-cheeked, chubby lad named Jochim led him into an office that did not have a name on its door, and that was some little walk from Shields's door, which not only had Shields's name on it, but SENIOR VICE-PRESIDENT as well. Jochim probably wasn't even a junior vice-president. But he was friendly and welcoming. For a while, at least. At the word "murder," his smile faded. He watched worriedly as Dave brought out a rumpled cargo manifest from his jacket, unfolded it, held it out.

Jochim read it, frowned. "But this was weeks ago."

"He didn't have a waybill for what he was hauling that night. Did it come from here? Could you check your files? Night of the ninth?"

"Why?" Jochim gave back the paper. "Why Tech-Rite?"

"It's someplace to start. The records, Mr. Jochim?"

"We've nothing to hide." Jochim touched an intercom button. "Shipping records for the ninth of this month." He tilted his head at Dave. "But surely this man hauled all sorts of cargoes, from all sorts of businesses."

"Not a lot that was dangerous," Dave said.

"Dangerous?" Jochim's voice squeaked like a high-school boy's. "What are you implying? We observe the strictest standards of safety in all our manufacturing processes. We have to. Most of our contracts come from the U.S. government. You've no idea of the restrictions they impose."

"That suggests that some of the materials that go into Tech-Rite products aren't exactly harmless."

Jochim drew breath to answer, and the door opened. The young oriental woman looked in. "I'm sorry, Mr. Jochim, but files from around that time are missing. No one in Shipping or Order has them. Shall we keep looking?"

Jochim raised pale brows at Dave. Dave shook his head. Jochim said, "That's all right, Frances. Forget it. Thank you." When the door closed behind her, Jochim said to Dave with a thin smile, "The environmentalists really make very little sense. Why would Tech-Rite or any of us manufacture products that would harm the very people we want to serve and serve again? Think about that."

"There was the asbestos business," Dave said. "And the coal-mining business. Not to mention the lead business. But okay. Even if what you make is harmless—poisons, pollutants, carcinogens come out of the manufacturing process, don't they? It's in the papers all the time. What does Tech-Rite do with its toxic wastes?"

"Just a damn minute." Jochim's face was red. "Are you holding Tech-Rite responsible for this trucker's death?"

Dave looked blank. "Why would you think that?"

"Then I don't understand your line of questioning," Jochim said. "And I don't like it."

"Let me explain," Dave said. He outlined the story of Paul Myers's lucrative, secretive, late-night hauling operations, the beating of Paul Myers's wife, the earlier recruitment of Myers by Ossie Bishop, the curious circumstances of Ossie Bishop's death. "I went down to Halcon to talk to his wife about it. She won't talk. She's frightened. But that I expected. What I didn't expect was that Ossie's truck was sold. For cash. In a great hurry."

"Yes?" Jochim asked warily. "To whom?"

"To a woman known as the Duchess. Ever hear of her?"

"Sounds like a cheap television show," Jochim said.

"Doesn't it? Unhappily, it's real. Why did she want that truck to disappear just when it was discovered that Paul Myers's death was no accident?"

"We farm out shipments to many independent truckers," Jochim said impatiently. "We really have no control over their activities, outside of their work for us. As for this missing truck—"

"I can't help thinking the Duchess wanted it out of the way because it contained evidence that would link Myers's death to that of Ossie Bishop. And I wondered what sort of evidence that would be. The truck was empty. Like Myers's. But law-enforcement laboratories don't regard 'empty' as the rest of us do. The Duchess must have been afraid traces of whatever Bishop was hauling at midnight in that truck were still there for electron microscopes to find."

"Are you suggesting that Tech-Rite—?" Jochim began.

"I read a disturbing article last night," Dave said. "In *Scientific American*. It describes the reactions of people who have handled toxic wastes carelessly. Violent diarrhea, vomiting, coughing, lung congestion, paralysis of the diaphragm—the same symptoms Ossie Bishop showed before he died."

"I see." Jochim gave a short nod and stood up. "Let me show you something. Can you spare me"—he looked at his wristwatch—"half an hour, forty-five minutes?" He didn't wait for an answer. He opened a closet, took out a pale raincoat, a rumpled rainhat. "I'm sure I can clear away all your doubts and dark suspicions." He smiled and opened his office door.

Dave smiled back. "Best offer I've had all day," he said, and followed Jochim out of the building. It was still raining in those fat, lazy drops, out of the sort of sky water-colorists like best, smudgy grays and whites. Beyond the hulking curves of the storage tanks, the mountains had already begun to show a tinge of green on their tawny summer hides. Dave walked beside Jochim into the executive parking lot. Coming out of the lot, hurrying in a clear plastic raincoat that rustled, a tall man nearly collided with them. Rain dripped from the brim of his rough Irish tweed hat as he glared at Jochim. The tall man was Lorin Shields.

"This is Mr. Brandstetter," Jochim told him. Dave wondered why the name seemed to startle Shields. Or was he imagining things? Jochim said, "He's an investigator for insurance companies. He's interested in our system of disposing of hazardous wastes. I thought I'd just show him."

"Good idea." Shields gave a brisk, executive nod, twitched a smile and tugged the brim of his hat to Dave, and loped off toward the bright doors of Tech-Rite.

Dave got into Jochim's Cimarron. "Your Mr. Shields looks like a man under a lot of strain."

"Lost his wife recently." Jochim drove down the long wet tarmac strip toward the gates. "Very suddenly. It was a shock. She was young. Beautiful. He worshipped her, built her a glorious new house. Married in April. Dead in September. Lorin hasn't collected himself. This place used to mean everything to him. Now he doesn't even come in, half the time."

The kitchen help, in rumpled, food-stained white jackets and pants, were eating when Dave stepped into Max Romano's through the back door. Steamy heat embraced him. The smells were overpowering—of garlic, cheese, fish, onions, basil, oregano. Alex, the skinny head chef with caved-in, acne-scarred cheeks, looked up from his plate of Alfredo and gave Dave his graveyard smile. The other men in puffed white hats—fish, soup, salad, dessert chefs—murmured welcomes. Dave pushed out a zinc-covered swing door into the quiet dining room. Max—short, fatter than ever, his few remaining curly locks combed glossily over his pate—was counting lunchtime checks by a tiny bright lamp at the cash register. Cocking an eyebrow at Dave, he turned back a snowy cuff fastened by a big diamond stud to read his watch, and shook his head in mock-fatherly reproach.

"You late again," he said. "Keep everybody waiting."

Dave laid a hand on his shoulder, then moved between white, empty tables to the corner table where Cecil sat. He gave him a kiss and sat down. "Sorry. I was treated to a demonstration of how scrupulous Tech-Rite is about dumping its toxic wastes." He laughed. "Or what was meant to be that." A little green bottle stood beside Cecil's wineglass. Perrier water bubbled in the glass. "You're not drinking?"

"I didn't know how long you'd be," Cecil said. "Didn't want for you to have to carry me out over your shoulder." He glanced through the shadows, looking for Max, but Max was already in the little bar. The restaurant was so quiet they could hear the clink of bottles, glasses, ice, that told them he was fixing their drinks. Cecil said, "What was it instead?"

"A farce." Dave told him the morning's events. "So we drove for twenty minutes to a place beyond beyond, with high fences and warning signs—a square mile of carefully labeled barrels of dangerous chemicals. And guess what? A picket line. All these men, women, adolescents, little kids, in jeans and parkas and slickers and stocking caps, carrying signs in the rain. Tech-Rite and the rest are poisoning the ground and water for miles around and dooming the people and their children for ages to come."

"Oh, wow! What did Jochim say?"

"He'd been lecturing me all the way how this was a government-approved dump. No danger of seepage, leakage, pollution. Tech-Rite and the others had gotten an order two years ago to clean it up and make it safe. It cost them millions—oh, grief, oh, sorrow. But now it was totally harmless." Max brought the drinks and set them down. Dave laughed again. "When Jochim saw those pickets, he stopped the car so fast it stalled. Then he dented the rear bumper, turning around to get the hell out of there."

"Was television covering it?"

"Men with cameras on their shoulders. Pretty girls of both sexes with microphones. Another reason Jochim stood not upon the order of his going." Dave grinned and picked up a chunky glass in which ice chilled Glenlivet. "Thank you, Max. What's left for lunch?"

"No leftovers." Max wagged disapproving jowls. "You tell me what you want, I fix with my own hands."

They told him, and he waddled away, singing to himself. Dave drank. "How did you fare at Chemiseal?"

"And Agroplex. I interviewed two merchants of death while you messed with one." Cecil pretended to preen. He drank, shrugged, made a wry face. "Guess that's what they mean by haste make waste. I didn't get anywhere."

"No one knew the Duchess?" Dave lit a cigarette.

Watching him wistfully, Cecil shook his head. "They let me see the shipping records. Paul Myers didn't haul for them the night he died." Cecil reached for Dave's cigarette pack on the white cloth, and drew his hand back empty. "They used Ossie Bishop, time to time. But when I raised the subject of toxic-waste disposal, the interviews were over. I sure as hell didn't get an all-expenses-paid, luxury vacation trip to the dump."

"Don't feel bad," Dave said. "Maybe they haven't got a dump."

13

The Valiant started reluctantly in the rain, but once all the cylinders began igniting in order, it followed the van without trouble back to Horseshoe Canyon. Dave had stretched lunch out, glad for the chance to rest, and it was ten past four when the van tilted ahead of him down the sharp drop from the trail into the bricked yard, and he jounced down after it. Rain still fell, dripping from shrubs, trees, eaves, and darkness was coming early. A four-wheel-drive sports wagon stood reflected in the front building's row of French doors. The vehicle was high on its wheels, well kept, three or four years old, with simulated wood paneling—and it looked empty in the rain.

But when Cecil rolled the van up beside it, Dave the jalopy, and the engines stopped and they got out, someone stirred in the wagon. A broad, black young face under a Padres cap looked out the driver's window. The door opened, Melvil Bishop got out. Three more faces appeared at the rear windows. Young boys' faces, somber. "Man, I was scared you'd never get here," Melvil said. "We been waiting for hours." He glanced at the small boys in the car. "They peed in your bushes. I'm sorry, but you know little kids. Always have to pee when it's no place for it."

"What are you doing here?" Cecil said.

"Where's your mother?" Dave said.

"Escondido," Melvil said. Rain was darkening the satiny fabric of the baseball cap. He moved away from the car, jerking his head to indicate that they should follow him. Out of earshot of the children, he said in a low voice, "Mercy Hospital. Critical condition." He glanced back at the car. All three faces were lined up at the rear window. Melvil said, "They don't know. They think she took sick. It wasn't that. She was shot."

Cecil sucked air through his teeth.

Melvil's eyes smoldered at Dave. "I knew something bad would happen when she told me she talked to you. We weren't supposed to talk."

"You mean the Duchess's goons shot her?"

"Sheriff say it was an accident." Melvil's tone was contemptuous. "First she talked to you. In the morning. Later on to Smithers." Melvil looked sharply at Dave. "Claim he work with you. It's a lie, isn't it?"

"It's a lie," Dave said. "I don't know him."

Cecil said, "Shot her at Hutchings's?"

Melvil shook his head. "You know the store in Halcon? General store? Post office? Indian dude run it?"

Dave stared. "The rifle range? A bullet from the rifle range?" He glanced at Cecil.

Cecil looked sick. "That almost happened to us."

"No 'almost' about this." Melvil's fists bunched in the pockets of his Padres windbreaker. His feet, in worn jogging shoes, nudged wet leaves on the bricks. He watched them. His voice wobbled. "She could die."

"I'll phone the hospital." Dave turned up his jacket collar and started off. "Collect your brothers and come inside." He took a few steps, then turned back. "Better get your car out of sight. Cecil, drive it up to Hilda Vosper's, will you?"

114

She was a neat little gray-haired widow who lived up the road with a feisty little ragbag dog, and had helped Cecil out of trouble once. "She only uses half her garage. She loves you—she'll let you hide it there." Cecil saluted, and Dave hunched his shoulders and hurried around the end of the front building, across the uneven bricks of the court-yard under the old oak, and into the rear building.

His desk waited at the far end of the long, high, plank-walled room. He sat at the desk and used the phone for a jokey, neighborly call to Hilda Vosper. Then he got to the process of connecting with the hospital down the coast. Before he managed it, Melvil came in, shepherding the small boys, two of them skinny, one stocky, a miniature Melvil. The room was gloomy, so their teeth and eye whites shone. They rolled their eyes. Plainly, they had never seen a place quite like this one. Come to that, neither had Dave.

"Cecil manage your car all right?" Dave called.

"Say he be back in a minute." Melvil shut the door. "Then he going to cook. These babies don't only always have to pee, they always hungry. He going to fix food for these here babies." Melvil gave the little boys quick, rough, affectionate shoves. "Don't push me, man," they said in small, high voices. "Look out who you messing with," the stocky one said. "I got me a big brother can beat the shine out of you."

"Where? Bring him on. I ready." Melvil scowled around him in mock truculence, and jabbed the air with blocky fists. The two skinny boys jumped on him from behind, clutching his shoulders, circling his neck, dragging him to the floor, where they piled on him and pummeled him.

At the Escondido end of the telephone line, a nurse, deceived by Dave's fast talk about insurance into believing he had a right to know, told him that Louella Bishop was in stable condition after surgery, though she was still uncon-

115

cious. Dave thanked the nurse and hung up. Melvil had heard his voice, and now sat up on the floor, brushing the giggling little boys off him, his eyes anxious. Dave rose, went to the broad fireplace, crouched there, and, with the aid of a gas jet, set kindling crackling and smoking under logs in the grate. Melvil came to him.

Dave got to his feet. "She's holding her own."

Melvil said darkly, "Why won't they sneak in and kill her in the hospital?"

"Intensive-care wards are busy places, filled with doctors and nurses," Dave said. "She'll be all right."

"I wanted to stay and guard her," Melvil said, "but they'd only kill me too. They know I know."

"If it's like that, why didn't you tell the Sheriff?"

"If Mama got shot for talking to you and Mr. Smithers, what do you think would happen, they see me talking to the Sheriff? Deputy phoned me at school, told me Mama had this accident, and could they come and get me, take me to the hospital? I say okay, but I didn't wait. I had the car. Mama used one of the Hutchingses' cars when she had errands. And I drove to the grade school and scooped up the babies and we came here."

"That's all right." Dave switched on lamps at either end of the long, corduroy-cushioned couch that faced the fireplace. "But I don't know why."

"Because Mama trust you. I yelled at her for talking to you. She say it's all right. You a fine man." He dug into his windbreaker pocket. "Gave me your card. Say if there was ever trouble, I was to get you." He showed the card. "I didn't know where else to go."

Dave looked at the little boys, who were playing tag up and down the pine stairs to the loft. He said to Melvil, "Why don't you take them to the cookshack? Then come

116

back here and tell me what it is they know you know."

"All I want is to hide," Melvil said.

"That won't work forever," Dave said. "Maybe if you had talked to Cecil yesterday, your mother wouldn't be in the hospital now. Maybe the sooner you tell what you know, the sooner you can stop hiding, the safer you'll be, and your little brothers and everybody else."

Melvil eyed him skeptically. "Insurance? What do you think you can do?"

Dave shrugged, smiled. "I sometimes surprise myself."

Melvil didn't look persuaded, but he rounded up the little boys and herded them, jumping and skittering, out into the rainy dusk. Dave made himself a drink and stood at the desk, listening to messages on his answering machine. Gene Molloy's voice, excited, exasperated. Salazar's voice, bored, exasperated. The voice of Amanda, his very young stepmother, widowed a few years back when Carl Brandstetter's heart stopped in his Bentley on a freeway. Amanda was cheery. She'd just got a new interior-decorating job and wanted to celebrate by taking Dave and Cecil to dinner. No more voices came from the machine. Dave reset it, lit a cigarette, picked up the drink, started for the couch, and the telephone rang. He sighed, sat down at the desk, picked up the receiver.

"You ought to stay home more," Salazar said. "Gene Molloy showed me those sketches of the brake system of a tractor-trailer rig that Kilgore drew. Kilgore doesn't look it, but he's weak. In ten minutes I had him in tears. And now I've got him in jail."

Dave raised eyebrows at the phone. "You mean he admitted blowing up Paul Myers? For Angela's half of the insurance money?"

"Not yet, but he will. He was read his rights, but he

117

babbled. He admitted he was planning it."

"Planning it is one thing," Dave said, "doing it is another." He took a quick gulp of whiskey. "What about Silencio Ruiz? Did you pick him up?"

Salazar's laugh was short, sharp, humorless. "That crazy old Gifford! You didn't tell me he's got a fortress out there. Electrified fence on top of the wall. Iron gates. Dogs that will tear your throat out."

Dave frowned. "Your men out there knew that."

"Yes, well, I didn't know it, did I? And Silencio is important to me. I got a warrant and went myself. And I blew it. No way was he going to let me in there. And no way was I going to risk ramming those gates. Those were little machine guns Silencio's boys took to the church barbecue. He could spray us with bullets from that tower."

"Right. So you staked the place out?"

"It's too big for that. We patrolled the walls. I did flyovers in the helicopter. It's got a spotlight on it to rake the ground, you know? Only with all those trees and bushes in there, what could we see? There's a loudspeaker. I kept telling Ruiz to come out, surrender. All it did was keep the old freak awake."

"He never sleeps much," Dave said.

"He complained anyway. This morning. When he came down in his wheelchair. To let us in. Holding up a pink Japanese parasol to keep off the rain. It was paper. It came to pieces while we watched."

"Did he have his rifle?"

"No rifle. You don't understand. He was a welcoming committee. I don't know what the hell he thought he was wearing. It looked like a glass bead curtain. 'Come in, come in,' he says. 'By all means, search the house and grounds. Freely. Take all the time you want. No need to worry about the dogs. I wouldn't let them out in the rain.'" Salazar snorted. "Sons of bitches were out in the rain all night, jumping at the walls, barking, snarling."

"Silencio got away," Dave said. "I hope when he went over those walls, The Edge wasn't watching."

"They were hanging around," Salazar said. "A crowd gathered when they saw all those County cars, all those spotlights, guns, uniforms. The noise of the chopper brought more. I saw Edge jackets."

Dave said, "Maybe he's still inside."

"No way," Salazar said. "We practically tore up the floor-boards. The place is a museum, did you know that? No, he escaped in the dark. I'd feel worse if it was the first stupid mistake I ever made. I'd feel better if it was the last. It was a great tipoff, Dave. Sorry."

"He didn't blow up Paul Myers," Dave said. "I don't think he led the raid on the barbecue. I believe the minister's wife. I think he tried to stop it."

"No way. Everybody was hysterical. I don't blame them. But witnesses are unreliable enough under normal circumstances. What am I saying? This is getting to be normal. Backyard terrorism. An American pastime."

"Bigger than divorce." Dave twisted out his cigarette and drank again. "No, I believe her because of something Gifford said—that prison changed Silencio. Gifford must have seen the G-G's from his tower, heading for the barbecue with their new guns, and told Silencio, and Silencio ran to try and stop them, and got there too late."

Salazar said, "Dave, Silencio Ruiz is human garbage."

"Probably literally, by now," Dave said. "The trash collectors will find him in a dumpster soon. That was why I wanted you to jail him."

"You don't think he killed Myers. You don't think Kilgore killed Myers. Who do you think it was?"

"I haven't got names," Dave said. "Only suspicions. Give

me a little more time, and I'll lay it on your desk."

"You always say that," Salazar said, "then you try to do it all by yourself. You can get killed that way."

Salazar had it backward. Dave never acted on his own, except when Salazar or Ken Barker of LAPD couldn't or wouldn't help. He didn't remind Salazar of this. He only said, "Tell me about it."

And Melvil came through the door, out of the rain.

14

He was eating a hamburger. Cecil made hamburgers with lots of mayonnaise, catsup, sweet pickle relish. The paper napkin in which Melvil's was wrapped was soaked with all these, and the juices of rare ground beef, tomato slices, onion slices. He came down the room through the circles of soft lamplight, the soft flicker of firelight, and laid another hamburger, swaddled in a napkin, on the desk in front of Dave, who nodded and watched it begin to ooze through the napkin while he wound up his talk with Salazar.

"Was Angela Myers in on Kilgore's plans for Paul?"

"Sorry to disappoint you," Salazar said. "That would lose her the insurance, wouldn't it—whether they actually killed him or not? Conspiracy to defraud? I questioned her. In my opinion, she didn't know Kilgore was using her. She's sick about it. She'll never speak to him again." At Salazar's end of the line, someone shouted his name in the background. "Listen, my wife's on the other line. I'll talk to you later. Don't do anything crazy, all right?"

Dave said he wouldn't, and cradled the phone. He regarded the hamburger on the desk and pushed it toward Melvil, who was standing, chewing, wiping mouth and fingers on his ruined napkin. Dave told him, "You have that one too. I finished a big lunch only an hour ago."

Melvil wrinkled his forehead. "You sure?" Dave nodded. Melvil tossed the crushed napkin side-arm down the room into the fireplace, where flames were lapping around the logs now. He picked up the second hamburger and lovingly peeled back half the wrapper. "That Cecil," he said, "make the best burger I ever tasted. Something about my people—what they cook taste better."

Dave grinned. "I taught him everything he knows. Bring that chair over and sit down." It was a wicker barrel chair. Melvil's stocky body fitted it exactly. "Who is the Duchess?" Dave said.

"I don't know her real name," Melvil said. "Don't guess nobody know that. She a broker. Work for factories that wants to get rid of poisons the cheap way. Hire truckers to take it off and dump it wherever they can. No questions asked."

"Did your Dad tell you this?"

Melvil looked ashamed. "I wanted to know what he was doing nights. We used to have good times together. Basketball games, Dodgers, boxing. All that stopped. Says with the new taxes and all that, he had to get more work. I don't know." Melvil shrugged, took a large bite from the hamburger. A scrap of lettuce pulled loose and hung at the corner of his mouth. He poked it inside. He spoke with his mouth full. "Was I mad at him, or jealous, or curious? Little of each, maybe. I wanted to be with him. He wouldn't take me. Course not." Melvil swallowed. "He knew how dangerous it was. Most truckers that did it—they knew. Acids to burn you, poisons to make you sick, fumes to make your eyes itch so you nearly blind, give you cancer, make your wife's babies come out deformed."

"And yet they do it?" Dave sipped his drink.

"The Duchess pay big bucks, man," Melvil said.

"He wouldn't take you. How did you learn?"

"Sneaked in the cab. They a big space behind the seat. Sometimes, some rigs, it living quarters, a bunk, all that. Hid myself back there. Saw it and heard it all. Scared me half to death. Dad never knew. I never said a word. I also never went with him again."

Dave lit a cigarette. "Where does this happen?"

"I'll show you, if you want to go there."

"A truck stop, rest area? Will the Duchess be there?"

"Sooner or later. This would be a good night. Raining. Not all that much traffic out late."

"If I were you, I'd be afraid," Dave said.

Melvil shrugged and munched his hamburger. A ring of raw onion tumbled down his front. He bent to pick it up off the floor. He carried it to the fireplace. "If it killed your father, you'd want to do something about it if you could, wouldn't you?"

Dave's drink was only ice now, no Scotch. He rose and went into the shadows where the bar was, and built a new drink. "A few minutes ago, you didn't think I could be of much help."

"Cecil told me about your track record." The firelight flickered orange-red behind Melvil. "You a real, live private eye. I didn't know they had those. You don't look it, you don't act it. You famous, too." He poked a last bite of hamburger into his mouth, wiped his mouth with the destroyed napkin, wiped his fingers, tossed the napkin into the flames. "Guess I should have known." He came back to the desk. The straw chair creaked under his weight.

"Did your mother know what your dad was doing?" Dave sat in his desk chair, high-backed, leather, swivel. "The Duchess seems to think so."

"I don't know what Mama knew. I got it together when

Paul Myers came over when Dad was sick and had that magazine article about the symptoms you get from handling toxic wastes, pollutants, all that jive."

"You overheard their talk?"

"I plain listened. Something those drivers said at the truck stop came back to me. I wasn't sure what it meant at the time. Then, when Paul talked about what was in that magazine, I understood."

"Your mother said Paul left the house angry."

"He was going to expose the Duchess and the whole rotten operation. That what he say." Melvil laughed wryly to himself and shook his head on its thick neck. "Folks talk big and bad, times like that. It the mob back of the Duchess, ain't it? Organized crime? What's some nobody truck driver going to do against organized crime?"

Dave said, "I think he meant it. I think he tried. He loved your father, you know. I read that magazine article. It must have been obvious to Paul from that, that your father was going to die."

"Tried how?" Melvil peered into the darkness behind Dave. "There water back there?"

"And glasses," Dave said, "and ice. Help yourself. There's a refrigerator under the bar, if you want a cola."

"Water be fine." Melvil pushed up out of the chair. "Cola rot you teeth and make you jumpy." He went into the darkness, silent on his soft-soled shoes. "Those babies—you think they grasshoppers now?" Ice clacked into a glass. Water drummed in a small steel sink. "Used to be they was into cola. Whoo. They was nonstop, eighteen hours a day." Melvil came back with the glass and sat down again. "What make you say he tried?"

"The Duchess brought her boys and beat up Paul's wife."

Melvil frowned, cocked his head. "Her? Not him? I thought they broke you legs."

124

"You can't drive a truck with broken legs," Dave said. "The Duchess preferred to have things both ways. Paul frightened into silence and still working for her. She managed that by abusing and threatening his family."

Melvil was staring gloomily at the fire. "Yeah. It wasn't herself Mama was scared for, taking off for Halcon that way right after the funeral. It was for us. Told me ten times a day, never say nothin' to nobody about what happened to Dad. None of it." His laugh was brief and bitter. "I wasn't about to. I knew more than she did, and what I knew scared me so I was afraid to go to sleep nights for fear I'd say something in a nightmare." He shook his head sorrowfully. "Turned out, she the one who talked. And look at her now."

Dave frowned. "It doesn't add up. The Duchess came for the truck. She got the truck. She went off with it. The night before Cecil and I talked to your mother."

"Then who fired at you from the rifle range?"

"Accidents have happened there," Dave said. "The storekeeper's dog was killed. That had to be a stray bullet. A customer was wounded, carrying sacks out to his car."

"The dog and the customer weren't trailing the Duchess," Melvil said. "Asking Paul Myers's widow questions. Drinking coffee with Ossie Bishop's widow."

"There's Smithers," Dave said. "Tall, bald, drives a Mercedes?" Melvil looked at him curiously and nodded. Dave added, "Did your mother tell you what Smithers wanted?"

"Pretty much what you wanted," Melvil said. "What was Paul carrying up in Torcido Canyon the night he got killed? Exactly where did he take it? Stuff like that." Melvil got out of the chair, went to stand looking at the fire. The flames had died down. There was a lot of smoke. He shifted the screen aside, found the poker, jabbed at the logs. Sparks flew up the chimney. "Oh, and about Ossie. He wanted to know did Ossie ever go up that canyon. See, he knew Ossie got Paul the nightwork."

"He learned that from Angela Myers," Dave said.

"What are you worrying about Smithers for?" Flames worked on the logs again. Melvil rattled the poker back into its glinting brass rack and hauled the screen once more across the rough brick hearth. "You think it was him shot at you, shot my Mama?"

"A man who goes around passing himself off as someone he isn't just naturally worries me. I know what the Duchess's stake is in all this. Where does Smithers fit?" Dave drank, scowled, chewed his lip. "How did he locate your mother? Angela didn't tell him—she doesn't know. Did he follow Cecil and me to Halcon?" On that long drive, had Dave been too concerned about Cecil to notice a conspicuous car trailing them, mile after mile? Shouldn't reflex have alerted him, a lifetime's experience? The years were catching up to him: he was losing sharpness. Annoyance at himself was in his voice when he said to Melvil, "What does Smithers want? Who is he?"

"Maybe he after the Duchess too." Melvil came back to the desk. He watched Dave light a cigarette. "You shouldn't do that. Ruin you lungs." Dave picked up his glass. "Alcohol too. Make you old before you time."

"It is my time," Dave said, and drank. "All right. To hell with Smithers. We'll go after the Duchess." He examined the boy's square, solemn face. "You really want to show me that truck stop? She's a deadly lady."

"You going to try to take her?" Melvil sounded awed.

"I'd prefer to leave it to the Sheriff. He has troops. I have a feeling troops are going to be needed. But you don't want anything to do with the Sheriff."

"If Mama die," Melvil said, "who going to look after those babies except me?" He laid a hand on the telephone.

"Do you think, if I was to get on here now and tell the Sheriff what I know, I'd still be alive to testify when they put the Duchess on trial?" He withdrew his   nd, sat down. His look at Dave was grave. "If it was a matter of troops, Mr. Bannister, how come she never been on trial yet? This been going on since before I was born. They never going to catch her. Nobody know who she is."

"Maybe we can find out." Dave rolled open a deep drawer of the desk, meant to hold files but holding cameras, binoculars, tape recorders. Elaborate and expensive equipment. None of which he had ever found a use for. "It will help to have a picture of her, won't it?" He lifted out a camera by the long strap on its case. "Something for me to show to Lieutenant Salazar, to accompany my description of the Duchess at work and play. Mine and Cecil's." He looked at Melvil. "Not yours. We'll keep you a secret." Beside the camera on the desk, Dave laid a camera-shop sack filled with little boxes. "How far away is this place? When should we start?"

Melvil peered into the sack. "You can't use these. Flash one bulb, everybody leave."

"Not those—this." Dave probed the sack and brought out a box of film and held it up. "Infrared-sensitive. For taking pictures in the dark." He unsnapped the camera case. "When do they meet at this truck stop?"

"Late. Midnight." Melvil watched Dave turn the camera over in his hands, frowning. Melvil said, "You don't even know how to get the film in there, do you?"

Dave held it out to him. The stocky boy put his hands behind him, shaking his head. "Don't ask me." He laughed. "This going to be some evidence-gathering expedition."

Dave set the camera down. "Cecil will know," he said.

The door flew open, and the small boys hurtled in. Two of them. The third, the chunky one, was riding on Cecil's

127

back. Cecil rolled his eyes. "Will somebody please take these monkeys off my hands?" The two skinny ones rattled up and down the stairs again, raindrops sparkling in their hair.

"Cool it!" Melvil shouted.

They came to a halt and stared at him. The chunky one slipped silently down off Cecil's back. They stood chastened. Melvil looked at Dave. "What we going to do with them? Do you know any baby sitters?"

"Amanda," Dave said, and reached for the phone.

Amanda said, "But I don't know anything about children."

"We were all children once," Dave said. "Some of us still are."

"Ah-ha!" she said. "I'll bring electronic games."

15

It was a lonely place, a long way from anywhere. Miles before they reached it, they saw the glow it made above the dark, rolling hills of the endless valley. When they did reach it, Dave drove on past. It was a black-topped acre or two, where the boxy hulks of tractor-trailer rigs loomed up against the lights of a filling station, a cinder-block motel, a glaring, glass-walled eatery. On the roof of the eatery, red neon spelled GOOD BUDDY. Plumes of smoke rose from the tall, plated exhaust pipes of some of the rigs. The rain laid a shine on the trucks, the paving, the jackets of men climbing down out of cabs, moving among fuel pumps, heading for or coming from the café. But the shine did nothing to change the bleakness of the place.

"There her van," Melvil said. "She here."

In the rear seat, the camera burred and clicked. Cecil had spent the evening hunched at Dave's desk, studying the instruction manual. He had fitted the camera with a night telephoto lens. At the time he bought the cameras, Dave had let the clerk sell him every sort of gadget and attachment. The motor traveled the film in the camera. Cecil clicked the shutter again. "Do you see her?" he said.

"No, but she there." Melvil twisted on the seat to peer back through the rain. "You want her license number."

Dave stretched across him, opened the glove compartment, took out pad and pen, dropped them in Melvil's lap. The boy held the pad close to his eyes and traced the numbers large and slow. "Look it up," he said, "find it belong to somebody dead, most likely."

Dave squinted past the batting wiper blades. "You picked the right night," he said, "but won't the weather keep her indoors? Won't she make her contacts in the café?"

"She work in the dark." Melvil stowed pad and pen in the glove compartment. "She don't trust but a few." The little door clapped shut feebly. "Where we going?"

"To find a side road," Dave said.

"Where would a side road go out here?" Cecil said.

"Maybe noplace," Dave said, "but we sure as hell are not going to drive into that truck stop and announce ourselves, now, are we?"

"She don't know this car," Melvil said. "Ain't that why we brought this car? Figure she know Ossie's car. Maybe she know Cecil's van. She don't know this car."

"She knows *you*," Dave said.

A truck lumbered out of the rest stop and onto the road. Its headlight beams glared in Dave's rearview mirror. He winced and moved the Valiant along faster. But very soon the diesel finished clashing its gears and roared up behind them. Dave looked for a wide, flat shoulder he could pull off onto. The headlights didn't show one. The diesel gave a blast of its air horn. Dave pulled onto a narrow, tilted shoulder and felt the rear wheels slide. The truck howled past, red lights glaring off its towering rear. The red lights dimmed and disappeared in the darkness and the rain. The Valiant stalled. It coughed when Dave tried to start it. But at last it started. He shifted into drive, and the rear wheels spun, whining.

"Oh-oh," Melvil said, and got out into the rain.

Cecil got out the back door. "Yuck," he said, "mud."

Dave stretched across the seat and looked out. He had turned off the headlights. Cecil and Melvil were almost invisible, a tall shape, a bulky shape in the blackness. Melvil lifted one foot, then the other. They came away with a sucking sound. "What do we do now, coach?"

"Should have brought Amanda's car," Cecil said. "Too light to get stuck." He didn't have a hat. He pulled his jacket up over his head.

"Too small," Dave said. It was an Alfa-Romeo two-seater. No room for his knees. Certainly no room for Cecil's knees. "There are three of us, remember?"

Cecil moved. "That's why we are all right." His voice came from farther off. "Two of us to"—he grunted— "push!"

"Not you." Dave got out of the car quickly and lunged for the rear, skidding in the mud, almost falling. The two leaned their weight against the trunk. Dave caught Cecil's arm. "You drive. You're in no condition for hard labor."

"Ah, listen, I'm okay," Cecil said.

"You want to go back to the hospital?" Dave said.

Cecil sighed and, with slumped shoulders, went and got into the car, behind the steering wheel. The whirling rear tires plastered Dave and Melvil with mud. But they got the old car onto the paving. And they found that side road. The trouble with it was that as it climbed into the hills, it veered away from the lights of the truck stop. Slithering and sliding, they backtracked.

"This is the closest point," Dave said. "Stop here."

"It quit raining," Melvil said. "That's nice."

Snagging themselves on barbwire fences, sometimes up to their ankles in mud, they slogged across farmland, uphill, toward the glow in the sky. Cecil's legs were longest and he led, camera case, equipment case, binocular case swinging from their shoulder straps, banging his lean hips. Breathing hard, muscles aching from the bad footing, they topped a ridge. Below lay the truck stop.

Dave unsnapped the binocular case. The view was good. A stout woman in a dark raincoat, a dark slouch hat shadowing her face, stood beside the high tractor of an eighteenwheeler, out near the edge of the shiny blacktop, where the light from the buildings was poor. A hulking man held a clear plastic umbrella over her, though the rain had stopped. In his other arm he cradled a stack of big brown envelopes wrapped in clear plastic. The long door of the truck cab opened and the driver climbed down, in a cowboy hat and dirty leather jacket. The woman passed him one of the envelopes. The binoculars were 7 x 50s with night lenses. Dave could see the driver's beard stubble, the pores under the woman's thick makeup. He handed Melvil the glasses.

"Is that the Duchess?"

"Where?" Melvil had trouble finding in the lenses that brought her close a figure that a moment before had been tiny. "Oh, yeah, that's her. See the big ugly with the stupid umbrella? He always with her."

"Probably the one who beat Angela Myers," Dave said.

From the darkness, Cecil said, "Damn," to himself. The camera churred and snapped. Again. Again. "Wish she'd take off that hat. Can't get her face. Now she's going to another truck. If she'd just once look up—"

"Don't worry about that," Melvil said. "Focus on the driver, man. Get pictures of what he going to do." Melvil nudged Dave's arm with the glasses. "Watch."

Dave watched. The man in the cowboy hat peeled the Saran Wrap off the envelope, dropped the wrap into an oily rain puddle at his cowboy-booted feet, tore open the flap of the envelope. He peered inside for a moment, reached inside, drew out thick white plastic sheets with raised red lettering. He reached up, slammed the door of the cab, hiked himself up, and flattened one of the sheets against the door: ACME WASTE DISPOSAL.

Melvil said, "Mama say you told her there ain't no Dr. Ford Kretschmer. Not in the phone book. Noplace. Well, ain't no Acme Waste Disposal, either. 'Peerless Sanitation' going to drive out of here tonight, too. Another one called 'Certified.' Names you might believe, if you didn't know the Duchess only made them up."

"Look at that." Cecil kept snapping the camera shutter. "Now it's a pirate ship."

Dave focused on the cowboy driver. He was slapping skull-and-crossbones warning placards on the trailer of his truck: HAZARDOUS CARGO. Dave lowered the glasses and frowned at Melvil. "I don't follow. You camouflage yourself as exactly what you are?"

"This only half of it," Melvil said. "He still got a lot of goodies in that envelope. You want to see how the last part work? We'll have to follow him."

"We can try," Dave said.

It was a grimy corner of L.A. At two-forty-five in the morning, the wet streets were empty. A freeway arched past, its trees and shrubs an unearthly green in the blaze of lights. Beyond the freeway, the glass towers of downtown glowed tall against the dark sky. Down here, there was a lot of shadow. The streets edged between old buildings, half of them blinded by plywood or rusty corrugated sheet iron. Dave held the Valiant back two blocks behind the giant semi, which bulked ahead of them almost as wide as the street. Red braking lights flared now on its rear. Its air brakes brought it to a hissing, clattering halt outside a brick wall where metal signs read MILLEX CORP.

Dave swung down a side street, then into an alley, to park between walls where graffiti was dense and as intricate as lace. Rain-soaked trash overflowed dented dumpsters and squished under the tires. The eyes of cats shone in the headlight beams and vanished. Dave switched off lights and engine. "That's a high wall," he said, and wearily pushed the door handle and climbed out. He left the alley and went back up the side street. The truck was inching through open gates into the Millex yard, which was now brightly lighted. Dave studied the street, then returned to the car and leaned at Cecil's window. "May I have the keys, please?"

Cecil pulled the keys out of the dashboard and handed them to him. Their little jingle was loud in the silence. Dave unlocked the trunk of the Valiant. The light was poor. He shone the sharp, thin little beam of a penlight into the trunk. A tire iron lay on the frayed carpet. He closed fingers around it and brought it out and slammed down the lid of the trunk. He pocketed the keys and started deeper into the alley. "Come on," he said, and heard them open car doors, scramble out, come hurrying after him. He played the little light along dank walls. The windows were high up and barred with iron. In sunken doorways, trash had accumulated against doors sheeted in metal, padlocked. He touched one or two of these padlocks, studied the slits of Yale locks, went on.

In the next block he found the kind of door he wanted. It was wooden. The hasp that held its padlock was rusty and hung a little loose off its screws. He wedged the tire iron under it, pushed. The screws came out and rattled in the litter underfoot. He didn't worry with the spring locks. He jammed the tire iron between door and frame and leaned his weight on it. Wood cracked and splintered. The tire iron slipped. Dave fell against the door. It gave, and he pitched into blackness. He fell, bruising elbows and knees on gritty concrete. The penlight skipped away. He dug out his cigarette lighter and flicked up a flame. The tube of the penlight glittered. Melvil picked it up and handed it back to him. Cecil helped Dave to his feet. "Stairs," Dave said.

They found a corner room on the third floor, empty, dusty, plaster fallen from the ceiling, where the view was good of the Millex yard. The window glass was dirty, and the lock on the window was corroded. Melvil hammered at it with the tire iron.

"Don't break the glass," Dave said.

"Hurry," Cecil said. "They're loading now." He had his face pressed against the next window. He rubbed at the grime on it with a hand, and shifted anxiously from foot to foot, and made small sounds of frustration while the camera, on its neck strap, jogged against his chest.

"Let me try," Dave said, and took the tire iron. He tapped it in under the window lock and pried. With a squawk, the lock came loose and flew in the air. Dave dropped the tire iron and pushed up the window sash. Cold, wet air came in. Cecil bumped against him and leaned far out the window. He began snapping the camera shutter again. Dave got the binoculars from the case on his hip.

Steel drums were stacked along a loading dock. Not many of them were new. A few had a little shine left to their finish, red, yellow, black. Most were mottled, pitted, streaked, colors no one could name. Wearing gauntlets and black rubber aprons, three men—two dockers and the driver—rolled the drums on dollies from the lighted platform into the dark trailer of the truck. A few drums bore faded company stickers, warning stickers. Not many.

"This a sleaze operation," Melvil said. "They don't care about nothing. Place Dad went did everything up neat, labeled what the chemicals were in the barrels, all that. Tech-Rite. They just as evil, but they make it look nice."

The loading took forty minutes. Then the driver shut down the door at the back of the truck, shoved the lock bolts to, and shed gloves and apron. A squat, paunchy docker dug under his apron and brought out folded papers. The driver unfolded these, read the top one, taking his time. He walked to a crate beside a door that gaped wide on a dim, empty storeroom, picked up his cowboy hat and put it on, laid the papers on the crate and signed them. The squat man took the papers back, separated the copies, handed a couple to the driver, folded the others and tucked them back under his apron. The other docker, a gaunt Latino with rounded shoulders, came out of the warehouse, carrying Styrofoam cups.

"Oh, no," Cecil groaned, and pulled himself back into the empty office. "They aren't going to drink coffee now." He peered at the elaborate black watch that made his wrist look fragile. "Don't we ever get to sleep?"

Dave heard his exhaustion. "Let's go," he said.

"Wait." Melvil took the binoculars. "It's not all over yet." He leaned out the wondow. "He ain't got time for coffee. Wherever he going to dump that stuff, it's a long way from here. He got to do it before daylight."

Dave touched Cecil's drawn face and returned to the window. The driver jumped down from the loading dock. He carried papers and coffee to the truck cab and climbed in. The big engine roared into life. Smoke poured out the high exhaust pipe. The brakes hissed, the gears ground. Jerkily, snorting, the truck nosed out the gates and lurched on big tires into the street. The space was narrow, so it took backing and filling, but at last the entire length of the rig was once more in the street. Headed back the way it had come. The yard gates swung to. A moment later, the yard went dark. The truck came on toward the building where Dave, Cecil, and Melvil waited. It stopped almost under their window. The driver climbed down, peeled the white magnetic signs off the doors, the skull-and-crossbones placards from the trailer.

"See?" Melvil whispered. "Now he nobody again."

The man climbed back into the cab. The angle from up here was steep, but Dave could see the man's hands sliding the signs back into the Duchess's brown envelope. He folded the posters and pushed them into the envelope too. He stuffed in the manifests given him by the Millex docker and drew out another set, green ones. These he stowed above his head, where Dave couldn't see. He dropped the brown envelope behind the seat and reached for the gear stick.

"Now he got cargo manifests he can show," Melvil said, "in case the CHP stop him or they a roadblock or something."

The brakes hissed. The big rig growled slowly off.

"Prepared by the Duchess," Dave said.

"Anything," Melvil said. "Stuffed toy animals."

"Paper hats for your end-of-the-world party," Cecil said, and began laughing and couldn't seem to stop.

Dave lifted the cases off him and draped them on himself. Cecil staggered with laughter. Dave took his arm and, by the gleam of the penlight, steered him toward the hall. "You're hysterical. Let's get you home to bed."

Melvil followed them, plaster crunching under his shoes. "Don't you want to see him dump it?"

"Not tonight, thanks." Dave's voice echoed in the stairwell. "Not unless it's up Torcido Canyon. Where Paul Myers went. That I want to see."

"Why didn't you say so?" Melvil said. "Torcido Canyon where Dad went that night I stowed away with him."

16

Cecil slept, slumped across the back seat, hands open in his lap, camera in its case in his hands. Melvil slept in the passenger seat, head over against the window, rolling against the glass with the movement of the car. The glass was wet. Rain had begun falling again about the time they reached Horseshoe Canyon. It was five o'clock but still dark. Dave ached from all the driving. He swung the Valiant gratefully down into the bricked yard and stepped on the brakes. The headlights shone on a patrol car, black and white, PROTECT AND SERVE on the door. Uniformed officers climbed out of the car, shining flashlights. One stood back, hand on the butt of a big revolver on his hip. The other came forward cautiously. He was young, blond, and looked sleepy.

"See some identification, please?"

"I live here." Dave dug the leather folder from his inside jacket pocket, flapped it open, held it out where the officer could shine a light on it. Plastic covered his badged cap. Rain beaded on his leather jacket. He squinted at Dave's private investigator's license. Dave said, "This is my house. What's the trouble?"

"You can put that away, thanks." The officer bent and shone his light inside. On Cecil. On Melvil. "Who are they?" He swung the light so it shone in Dave's eyes. "Are you all right? What's the situation here?"

"You mean," Dave said, "they're black and I'm white, they're young and I'm old, so something must automatically be wrong?" He pushed the door handle and moved to get out. The officer didn't step back. Dave jerked his head to indicate Cecil. "And he is surrounded by rich men's toys?"

"This car is no rich man's toy." The flashlight played over the dented thin-gauge steel. "Guess I'm a little confused."

Cecil stirred, lifted his arms to stretch, stopped and sat up straight. "What's going on?"

"Just keep your seat, please," the officer said.

"The car is a cover," Dave said. "For stakeouts. That young man is Cecil Harris, my associate. He lives here. This is Melvil Bishop. I'm looking into the death of his father. He's helping me. He's my houseguest."

Melvil opened his eyes. "Oh-oh," he said.

Dave asked the officer, "What are you doing here?"

"Mrs. Brandstetter called us. Prowler with a gun. Tried to make her let him in. When she refused, he sat out here in his car." The young man smiled slightly. "Rich man's toy. A new Mercedes. By the time we got here, he was gone. Smithers. You know a Smithers?"

"Nobody knows Smithers." Dave pushed the door a little farther open. "Not by that name. Excuse me—I'd like to get out of the car now." The officer took two steps back. Over beside the black-and-white, where a radio dispatcher's voice crackled quietly, the other officer kept his hand on his gun. Dave got out into the gentle rain. "Smithers is involved somehow in a case I'm working on for Pinnacle Life. That's all I know."

"Your wife," the officer said, "seems to think he came to kill you."

"Is she all right?" Dave said.

Melvil leaned across the seat. "What about the babies?"

"She's worried for you," the officer said. He frowned at Melvil. "She didn't mention any babies."

Melvil scrambled out of the car. The officer by the patrol car drew his gun. "My little brothers," Melvil said, turned, and took steps across the wet bricks.

"Hold it right there," the officer with the gun said.

And Amanda came through the headlight beams, small and trim, cinching the belt of a red raincoat. Her dark eyes were wide with worry. "Thank God you're back," she said, and put her arms around Dave and laid her neat head against his chest for a moment. She looked up into his face. She was pale. "Are you all right?"

"Fine," he said. "I'm worried about you."

"I'm unscathed," she said. "Just scared witless."

"What about my brothers?" Melvil said.

"Asleep." Amanda gave him a weary smile. "And if they sleep as hard as they play Donkey Kong, they'll stay asleep for a while."

"You right about that." Melvil laughed relief.

"You know Bishop here?" the officer asked Amanda. "Harris, in the car there?"

"Yes, they're friends." Amanda nodded.

"And this *is* your husband?"

Amanda blinked at Dave, mischief in her eyes. She was about to complicate things. Dave wanted to sleep. He shook his head at her pleadingly. She sighed, looked at the officer, and said, "Yes, of course. Thank you for staying. I'll be all right now."

"You're welcome." The officer touched his cap. He

looked at Dave. "Two other patrol cars searched the area. No sign of Smithers. We ought to locate him. Forty to fifty years of age? Tall—six three or four? Slender—hundred sixty-five pounds?"

"Bald?" Dave said.

"He was wearing a hat," Amanda said.

The officer asked Dave, "Sure you can't help us?"

"If I learn anything," Dave said, "I'll call you."

Tapping woke Dave, the sharp rap of a finger ring against glass, one of the square panes of the door from the court-yard into the front building. He didn't make a lot of use of the front building, though Amanda had made it handsome. He entertained in it. It had the best sound system, so he sometimes did his listening here. Otherwise he rarely entered the place.

But last night Amanda had put the little Bishops in the bed on the loft in the back building—the only bed in the place. So Melvil had slept on the one couch in the back building. And Dave and Cecil had slept on couches up here.

Daylight, gray and rainy, but daylight, came into the big, raftered place through clerestory windows above a cur-tained row of French doors. Dave turned on the couch, stiff, aching, fumbled on the floor for his watch, and squinted groggily at the time. Not yet ten o'clock. Clutch-ing the blanket around him, he sat up and peered.

A big-shouldered man was doing the rapping. Not a tall, thin man. Dave shrugged off the blanket and, shivering in briefs and T-shirt, kicked into trousers and pushed as creak-ily as old Reverend Prentice up off the couch. He crossed deep carpet, climbed a level, unchained and unbolted the door, opened the door to cold dampness.

"Ken," he said. "What is this?"

"Sorry to wake you." Rain dripped from the crumpled canvas hat of Captain Ken Barker, homicide division, LAPD. He had a broken nose, and eyes the same dark gray as the clouds that hung low over the canyon this morning. "But I understand a man came by last night to murder you. It awakened my protective instincts."

"Come in," Dave said. He rubbed his forehead. There was an ache there. Barker stepped in, dripping, and Dave shut the door. It closed with a stutter against the sill; the rains had swollen it. "Let me take your coat and hat." Amanda had stationed a coat rack by the door. Dave hung Barker's mac on it, hat stuffed in the pocket. "I didn't get to bed until six." Dave moved down into the room. "What else did you hear?"

"Westside went to work on Smithers." Barker followed, lighting a cigarette, watching Dave, who sat on the couch again, picked up socks, found them damp and muddy, didn't put them on. Barker said, "No Smithers owns any Mercedes—not in California. Why didn't your lady get the license number?"

With slow, mindless motions, Dave folded the blanket. "Because, when it rains too much, the landscape lights in front short out. I keep forgetting to get them fixed."

From down the room came Cecil's voice: "Oh, man, do you know what time it is?" His head appeared above the back of the couch. He looked as cranky as he sounded. "We just got to sleep. Why do you want to start so early?" He saw Barker. "Oh, sorry."

"Who are you?" Barker said.

"You got older," Dave said, "and they made you a captain and gave you more help. I got older, but I had to round up my own help." Cecil came from the couch, yawning, shuffling, wrapped in his blanket. Dave introduced them. They shook hands. Cecil's blanket slipped off his shoulders. The scars showed on his ribcage. Barker recognized them for what they were and frowned.

"Where did you get those?" he said.

Cecil pulled up the blanket. "Line of duty," he said. "You going to find Smithers?"

"He never registered that gun," Barker said.

"It's not his real name," Dave said. "The case we're working on is full of phony names—individuals, companies." A coffeemaker was behind the bar. He loaded it and set it to work. Then he started the signal going on an intercom he had never used. Barker blinked. "We need dry clothes," Dave explained.

"Out in the rain all night," Cecil said.

"What kind of case?" Barker said.

Dave told him about the Myers case—omitting the parts involving Ossie Bishop and family. "Smithers appeared after the newscasts about the bomb. He didn't realize I'd already been to see Angela Myers, and he tried to pass himself off as an investigator for Pinnacle Life."

The beeper stopped. Melvil's voice came from the intercom, cottony with sleep. "I'm sorry. I couldn't find it. Looked high and low. How come you hide it?" Dave remembered only now that he had cleared the intercom in the back building off the desk as superfluous weeks ago and stowed it on a bookshelf. "Woke the babies up too."

"They've had their sleep," Dave said.

"That's just the trouble." The voices of the little boys were shrill in the background. "They got cartoons on up there. Use your bed for a trampoline."

"We'll feed them," Dave said, "just as soon as you bring over dry clothes for Cecil and me."

"I didn't hear the phone ring," Melvil said. "So they ain't no news about Mama?"

Dave read his watch again. "Amanda should be at the hospital by now, unless the traffic was bad. She'll be calling soon."

"Hope so. Those babies going to miss Mama pretty quick now. They all start crying together, you never heard nothing like it." Melvil sighed. "All right—I'll bring you clothes." The intercom went silent.

Dave found mugs under the bar. He said to Barker, "Mrs. Myers was at work." He peered into the mugs. Dusty. He rinsed them at the little bar sink. "But her brother was at home. All muscle and gut. Bright enough to guess Smithers was lying, but dumb enough to show off how smart he was by flashing my card."

"And letting Smithers walk off with it," Cecil said.

"Pinnacle never heard of him?" Barker said.

"You should be a detective." Dave dried the mugs with a starchy little towel and set them on the bar. They looked good—hand-thrown, with a drizzly brown glaze. Expensive. Of course. Amanda had chosen them. "We'll have some coffee here shortly."

"Good." Barker leaned on the bar. "Is your lady sure he came to kill you? Or did she jump at that when she saw his gun?"

"Let me tell you how it went." Dave took the cigarette pack from the breast pocket of Barker's whipcord jacket. "I've got a client staying here." Lighting a cigarette, Dave nodded at the intercom. "The boy whose voice you just heard. Also his three little brothers."

"Name of Bishop," Barker said, taking back his cigarette pack, tucking it away. "I read the report."

"Then you know Amanda was babysitting while Cecil and

I took Melvil with us on this stakeout."

"I want to hear about the stakeout next."

Dave shook his head. "No, you don't. It's not your worry. It connects to the Myers matter, and that's County, not City. I promised to lay it on Jaime Salazar's desk. I'm going to do that this morning—for what it's worth."

"Smithers came here." Barker stubbed out his cigarette in a brown pottery ashtray on the bar. "This is City."

"Amanda had tucked the kids in." Dave tilted his head. "You've been here. You know the layout."

Barker nodded. "Loft in the rear building."

"And she thought she'd like to relax with television," Dave said, "and she didn't want the kids to wake up again, so she turned down the lamps back there, put on her raincoat, and started for this building."

"And she saw a guy skulking around with a revolver," Barker said, "and she was closer to this building by then, so she ran for it."

"And he saw her," Cecil said, "and chased her."

"He didn't shoot at her," Barker said.

"It was me he wanted to shoot." Dave took the pot and filled the mugs. "Amanda and I don't look alike—not even in the dark." He set the pot back in place.

"She locked and bolted the door there." Barker's somber eyes measured the door, unhappy at all those glass panes, thick though they were, and even though the old wood that clinched them was heavy and strong. "And she very sensibly did not turn on the lights."

Dave slid one of the mugs at him. "She started for the phone over there. To summon your people."

"But he banged on the door." Cecil came to the bar, still wrapped in his blanket. "And gave his name—if that is his name." He was tall enough to bend far over the bar and peer beneath it. "Sugar?" he asked Dave. "Cream?"

146

From the little refrigerator Dave brought a brown pottery sugar bowl, a cold spoon leaning in it. "Afraid you'll have to rough it." He showed Cecil a blue pint carton. "This cream is dated two months ago."

Making a face, Cecil spooned sugar into his coffee.

Barker said to Dave, "So he yelled through the door that he had to see you. It was urgent. He knew you were here because your car was here. He meant the van out there with the flames painted on it." Barker gave the semblance of a laugh. "He doesn't know you very well."

"It's Cecil's van." Dave tried his coffee and it made him feel better right away. "I drive a brown Jaguar these days. It's in the repair shop for the moment."

"She insisted you weren't here and told him to go away and he went away," Barker said, "but only out to his car, to wait for you to show up. That's what bothers me. He had to know she'd call the police."

"He wasn't here when they got here," Cecil said.

Barker nodded, frowned, worked on his coffee. "But it's as if he meant to be. At first. Then changed his mind. That's puzzling." With a thick finger, Barker dug out his cigarettes again, extended the pack to Dave, to Cecil. Dave's cigarette still burned. Cecil wanly shook his head. Barker's lighter was an old Zippo, embellished with a small police badge in worn gold and silver. He lit his cigarette and put pack and lighter away. He lifted his coffee mug and frowned at Dave over it. "Has it occurred to you that Smithers might be an investigator? Federal, state? Even County? The grand jury's investigating the illegal dumping of toxic wastes."

"If the grand jury wants me," Dave said, "sending a prowler with a gun in the middle of the night seems an odd way to go about it."

"And that isn't all," Cecil said. "That same man—"

Dave reached to clap a hand over Cecil's mouth, when the door opened and Melvil came in with an armload of clothes wrapped in dry-cleaning-shop plastic. "I didn't know what you needed, so I brought everything I could think of." Melvil looked around the big, comfortable, multilevel room. "Where shall I put them?"

"Thank you," Dave said. "On that couch is fine."

Barker turned to watch Melvil carry the clothes to the couch and lay them down. Behind Barker's muscular back, Dave frowned at Cecil and put a finger to his lips. Cecil showed bewilderment, but he gave a shrug of acceptance. The blanket slipped off his shoulders again. He pulled it up.

"This plastic wet," Melvil said, and began to unwrap the clothes. "Listen, those babies want breakfast. Be all right with you, if I was to—?" The telephone rang. It sat on a table at the end of the couch. Melvil didn't wait for Dave. He stepped to the phone and picked it up. He started to say "Hutchings," but caught himself and said, "Bannister residence," instead. Then he listened. It was quiet in the room. The rain pattered on the roof, splashed on the bricks outside, pinged on the parked cars. Melvil's face lit up. He put a hand over the mouthpiece and said, "She all right. My mama going to be all right." He said into the phone, "Mama? How you doing? No, they fine. We all fine. Mr. Bannister looking after us. I will. I'll thank him. I want to see you too. Soon as it safe. Won't be too long now. You take it easy, hear me? I be calling you." He put the phone into Dave's hand.

"Amanda?" Dave said.

"She saw the man who shot her," Amanda said. "He stepped from behind the store. It was Smithers."

17

After he had delivered the film to Salazar, along with his clumsily typed report of last night's watch—bearing his own fingerprints in bacon grease because he had been too hungry to forgo breakfast, and in too much of a rush not to work while he ate—after he had delivered these, he didn't wait around. The Jaguar was ready. The agency had telephoned just as he was going out the door of the back building in Horseshoe Canyon—or trying to go out the door, hobbled by Melvil's giggling little brothers clinging to his legs. From the Sheriff's, he drove out the Santa Monica Freeway to Beverly Hills, the junkyard car developing croup as the wet miles passed. He left the snooty dealership the embarrassment of returning the Valiant to his house, and himself drove the Jaguar to a gun shop.

It stood on a quiet street in West L.A., in a row of shops climbed on by vines that gave them a cozy look. Knitting yarn should have been sold in this one, or dolls. The place was hushed by carpeting. The paneling looked almost real. Gentility seemed to be the aim. The salesman wore a quiet, high-priced, three-piece suit, a handsome white mustache, an English accent. His coloring harked back to that old rhyme about the good roast beef of England. He was affable and ready to chuckle. He was selling death.

Dave let him place on top of a glass showcase several brands of death—Colt, Smith & Wesson, Browning—snubnosed .38 Detective Specials, the .45s favored by television cops. Dave hefted them by turn, let them nestle cold in his hand. The man found good and bad to say about each one, his bloodshot blue eyes watching Dave closely, sensitive to the slightest signal of acceptance or rejection. To relax the man, Dave said the gun should be simple and reliable, and be able to shoot many times without reloading. The cost didn't matter.

He walked out onto the dripping, tree-lined street with a Sig Sauer nine-millimeter automatic, pride of the Swiss army, able to fire eight thousand rounds in the field without a hitch. It held thirteen rounds in the clip, one in the chamber, cost five hundred fifty dollars, and rode snugly in a Bianchi holster against his left ribs. He would never be comfortable with it. He had never wanted a gun. For decades he had managed without one. But times had changed. The game he loved had turned lethal. People kept trying to kill him and his.

As he unlocked the Jaguar, folded himself into its comfort, started the quiet, powerful engine, listened to it purr, the notion came to him again that had surprised him often lately—that he ought to quit. That would be sensible. He wasn't getting any younger. He didn't need the money; his father had left him a great many shares of Medallion stock. But sensible was boring. What the hell would he do with his days and nights? He grimaced, read his watch, looked in the side mirror for a break in traffic, swung the Jaguar in a fast U-turn, and headed back to Horseshoe Canyon to pick up Melvil.

The spur of Torcido Canyon to which Melvil pointed him would have been easy to miss. Its road was a narrow strip of blacktop that the rain had damaged. It followed a crooked creek along the bottom of a canyon whose walls went up steeply, covered in dry brush showing new tips of green, with occasional clumps of live oak and outcrops of rock. The ridges were high above. The creek ran rough and swollen among boulders and twisted white sycamores hung with scraps of yellow leaf.

"Hard to imagine a semi negotiating this road," Dave said. "How much farther is this dump?"

"Dad, he took it real slow, change gears a lot." Melvil frowned ahead through the afternoon rain. "Not too far now. Look a little different in the daytime."

"You sure you can find it?"

"I think so. Yeah. There. See that turnoff?"

The Jaguar scraped bottom, following ruts carved by the giant tires of tractor-trailer rigs. Oaks grew large and close here, very old. The wheels of the Jaguar slurred in mud and wet grasses. And here was the dump, in a declivity circled by dead ferns. Filled with steel drums like those they had watched trucked out of Millex last night—this morning. Tumbled there, labels peeling, rusting in the rain.

"Smell it?" Melvil put a hand over his nose and mouth. "Make you sick, you breathe that for long." His eyes clouded. He turned his face away. "Worse than sick. Kill you." He whispered. "Killed my daddy."

"I need the camera," Dave said, and got out of the car. The smell was strong, caught in his throat, stung his eyes. Melvil pulled the camera from the glove compartment, lay across the seat, handed it out to Dave. "Thanks. I'll make it quick." He fiddled with the camera, uncertain, hoping he was making the correct adjustments for the poor light. He took twenty shots, got back into the car, passed the camera to Melvil. He slammed the door, started the engine. "What a nightmare," he said. He pressed the throttle, and the rear wheels spun.

Melvil sighed. "One more time," he said, and got out into the rain to have a look.

Dave got out too. "I'm a slow learner," he said.

"Be all right," Melvil said, and looked around him. "If we can find something to put under the wheels." He made a face. "Don't like touching nothing here." He rubbed his hands on his pantlegs. "How about this?" He took a few steps, slipping a little in the mud, then bent and heaved up from among the brittle, rust-brown ferns the end of a four-by-four, six feet long. He wrestled it loose from creepers that had gripped it. They were dead and dry too. The end of the timber came loose with a ripping sound.

A signboard was bolted to that end. Melvil wrestled the four-by-four toward the car. "'No dumping,'" he said. "How about that?" With a disgusted laugh, he let the post drop behind the car. Dave went to help him. Muddy-handed, they wedged the four-by-four under the rear wheels. Halfway back to the road, the rear of the car slewed and the wheels mired again. They hiked back for the post. In small print across the bottom of the sign were numerals from a County ordinance book. And below that, TORCIDO CANYON HOMEOWNERS ASSN.

Back in the car, inching it warily along the muddy ruts, Dave said, "No homeowners in this part of the canyon."

"Up there." Melvil sat forward on the seat, peering upward through the glass. "One. Look new to me."

It hung two hundred feet above them on the brushy canyon wall, all alone, raw cedar and tall glass, sharp roof angles, decks thrusting out like bony wings. Tall pin oaks grew around the house. It looked beautiful in the sifting rain—a picture for an architecture magazine. But there was something desolate about it.

Dave checked his watch. No time to go up there. Salazar expected him at four. He'd be late as it was. The Jaguar lurched heavily onto the potholed blacktop of the trail. He drove it as fast as he dared, the tires spraying water at places where the creek overflowed onto the paving. He skidded at the boulevard stop where the spur canyon opened on Torcido Canyon road. The spur canyon had a name—Concho.

Darkness was coming early again. The shift was changing. Men were leaving the squad room in dry raincoats. Men in damp raincoats were coming on duty. They brought whiffs with them of the moist air of the streets, the smell of rain on sidewalks. Phones rang. Voices spoke, laughed, swore. Typewriters rattled. From outside, above the steady growl of home-going traffic, sirens wailed and faded.

"Who led you into this?" Salazar looked and sounded pained. His hand slapped a stack of papers in front of him. "Do you realize how big this is? And how nasty?" Dave blinked at him. Salazar said, "What took you in? And I don't mean the Myers matter."

"An informant." Dave hung his raincoat on a hook by the door of the glass box that was Salazar's office, off the squad room. "On the understanding that I wouldn't disclose his name or whereabouts." He sat down facing Salazar across the desk. "The pictures came out, then?"

"The pictures are lousy. You can't take telephoto pictures without a tripod. Handheld is too jittery." Sourly, Salazar passed the pictures across. They looked as if they had been taken at night in the rain. "But he got one that wasn't too bad. Even with the hat."

"Of the Duchess." Dave studied it.

"We got responses on that from all over the state, all over the country. Clara Blodgett, née Leopardi. In twenty-five years, eleven arrests, no convictions."

Dave handed back the pictures. "Why? Her operation depends on a great many people she can't really know well enough to trust."

"She doesn't trust them. She scares them."

"She ever blow anybody up before?" Dave said.

"Maybe." Salazar thumbed through the papers. "Your license number didn't lead us anywhere. Belongs to a car junked years ago. Owner, no connection."

Dave laughed wryly. "My witness thought the owner would be dead."

Salazar said, "Sounds like he knows her. Don't feel bad. Even if we located her and took her to trial, nobody would testify against her. They got a witness once in—where? Florida? Texas? I forget." He scowled at the papers, sat back, gave his head a dismissive shake. "Doesn't matter. They registered him under a false name in a motel. Officers around the clock, eating with him, sleeping with him. They didn't go to the bathroom with him. Somebody shot him through the bathroom window. But mostly, by the time law enforcement gets a line on a witness, the poor bastard is already dead—accident, suicide. You know."

Dave reached across and touched the papers. "In all of that, did you run across an associate of hers, a hitman maybe, named Smithers? Using that name, that alias?"

"I spent the whole day with this file." Salazar found a flat box on his desk, lit a thin brown cigarette. "I'd have noticed that." He pushed the papers around for a minute, regarded Dave through blue smoke. "Smithers? Smith? That's a dumb alias."

Dave lit a cigarette of his own. "So you're saying I wasted a night and risked pneumonia for nothing? She can't be touched?"

"You get this witness of yours to drive a truck there, get an assignment from the Duchess, the signs, the warning stickers, the phony documents, the trailer full of chemicals, and bring them all to us, and—"

"She already wants him dead," Dave said. "His mother's been shot. I sent Amanda down there. The woman told her it

154

was Smithers. San Diego County's got deputies in the hospital now, guarding her."

Salazar went straight on: "And even then, we'd haul fat Clara in, she'd have a high-powered lawyer with her, be out on the street in an hour, and when it came to trial in a couple of years, there'd be ten witnesses that she wasn't even there. Nobody at the truck stop would talk. Who wants to end his life wrapped up in razor wire? As for the company that shipped the stuff—maybe they'd get fined a few thousand bucks for illegal dumping. And they'd be right back at it the next week."

"My witness heard Paul Myers say he was going to expose the Duchess." Dave stretched to use the ashtray. "You know what happened. Myers's wife was beaten up, and when that didn't work, Myers was killed."

Salazar swiveled in his chair to gaze at the rain running down his window. "The witness, Dave."

"Give me back my report." Dave rose wearily. "And the pictures. I'll turn them over to the grand jury. I'll testify to the grand jury."

Salazar swiveled around and gazed up at Dave with pity. "They'll jail you for refusing to divulge your source. And if you get out of jail alive, you'll turn the ignition key to start your car, and blam! Instant cremation. No waiting." He slipped the envelope of photographs from the stack of papers, along with Dave's typed pages fastened with a paperclip. "Here you go." He passed them over. "But don't do it. It's not worth it."

"It might save some lives," Dave said. "This is going on all over the country, been going on for decades. They make more and more laws against it, federal, state, local. Talk about it, write about it, but it just gets worse." He went for his coat. "The air is poisoned, ponds, rivers, lakes, whole oceans. The water under the land. The land itself. Farms, the animals on the farms. People. Whole towns have to be abandoned.

155

Somebody has to stop it." He shrugged into the coat.

Salazar came to take down his own coat. "Did you see that picket line out at the Foothill Springs dump? They had it on TV." He put his coat on.

"I saw it in person." Dave folded the useless photos and report and jammed them into a pocket.

"Yes, well," Salazar said. "It will be them that stop it, Dave. Not you. Not the grand jury. The grand jury has been promising a report for months. It never comes." Salazar opened his door. The noises of the large room—telephones, typewriters, voices—were suddenly loud again. He led the way between busy desks. "Why don't you forget it, and do something you can do? Sign the papers on the Myers case and get the widow her check." He opened another door, and they were in a bright hallway. "Whoever killed him—the Duchess or Silencio or Kilgore—he's just as dead. And she can use the money. She's got kids."

"Also a sick old father," Dave said. "Damn it, I wish the man hadn't been hauling dangerous cargo. On that two-year conditional clause, Pinnacle won't pay her a dime."

"The truck was empty." Salazar pushed a wall button to bring an elevator. "Why isn't that enough for them? You don't have to tell them everything you know." The elevator doors opened. Two uniformed women stepped out. Salazar stepped in, waited for Dave, pushed a button. The doors slid shut. The elevator moved. "You don't really know much, the way I see it. Not that you can prove."

Dave smiled bleakly. "I've made a lot of trouble for a lot of people. It would be pretty sad if it all added up to nothing."

"You're not going to quit. Right?" Salazar said.

"I guess I don't know how," Dave said.

18

The little Bishops slept in the big bed in the loft again. Cecil had stuffed them with lasagne Bolognese until they nodded. "They liked it better than Spaghetti-O's," Melvil said. Melvil was in the back building with them. Cecil had lent him a big portable radio and cassette player. Wearing headphones, and wrapped in blankets because it was another cold, wet night, Melvil lay on the long corduroy couch in front of the fireplace where logs flamed low, and listened to Blondie. He could watch the door from the couch. It was bolted and chained, but he was afraid, just the same. Of Smithers.

In the front building, Dave sat relaxed with a drink on another couch, facing another fire. Cecil lay stretched out on the couch, his head in Dave's lap. The sing-along recording that Glenn Gould had made of the Goldberg variations just before his death was on the turntable. No light was in the room except that from the fireplace. The gain was low on the stereo equipment. Dave wanted to be able to hear cars on the trail. Passing, he hoped. Of course, if Smithers came back, his headlights would swing across the clerestory windows. But only if he left his lights on. He might not do that.

The Sig Sauer automatic lay on Cecil's belly. Its bronze metal gleamed in the firelight. His hands rested on it. He

157

grumbled, stirred, laid the gun on the floor, out of sight. "You want me to say it's a beautiful piece of machinery?" Dave didn't answer. Cecil was quiet for a long time, touching whiskey to his mouth from a squat glass in which ice trapped the color of the flames. "Ought to be," he said. "Cost enough." Dave made a noncommittal sound and absently traced a fingertip over the intricacies of one of Cecil's tight little ears. "Man who trained me with the targets at LAPD," Cecil said, "told me that in this country law enforcement says a .45 stops a man best. But in Europe it's the nine-millimeter. Don't you love thinking about the kind of research that went into forming conclusions like that?" He touched the glass to his mouth. "They could have used me—if I'd just been a little deader."

Dave laid fingers on his mouth. "Please," he said.

"I don't want to shoot anybody," Cecil said.

The telephone rang. It was at Dave's elbow. He picked it up, grateful he'd remembered to unplug the two instruments in the rear building. The little Bishops would sleep on. "Brandstetter," he said.

"They're breaking in here." The voice was hoarse, quiet, shaky, distorted because the mouth was too close to the instrument. "They've cut off the electricity. The alarms aren't working, the electrified fence."

"Gifford?" Dave frowned at the phone. "What are you talking about? Who's breaking in?"

"The Edge, of course," Gifford snapped. "That black gang. I don't know what's happened to the dogs. They raved and raved, and now it's silent out there."

"What does The Edge want with you?" Dave didn't need to ask. "It's not you. It's Silencio, isn't it? Ruiz. He's there with you."

"Of course. You know that. You knew it all along. You've protected him as much as I have. We had an understanding, didn't we? No need for words—not between us. You'll help me now. I know you'll help me now." Something crashed in the background. "No, wait! Silencio!" A voice spoke, but too far off for Dave to make out what it said. Gifford had the phone to his mouth again. "They are on the porch. They're breaking down the doors."

"Phone the Sheriff," Dave said.

"How can you say that? You know what the Sheriff will do to Silencio. Are you coming to help me or not?"

"I'll be there," Dave said. He hung up. "Got to go," he said, and lifted Cecil's head. "Get hold of the Sheriff substation in Gifford Gardens—or whichever one is nearest Gifford Gardens." Dave went down the long, shadowy room for his raincoat. "Send them to De Witt Gifford's. Someone's trying to break in." Dave flapped into his coat and unbolted the door. "He thinks it's The Edge. Since he's got Silencio with him, I wouldn't be surprised." Cecil came to him, holding out the Sig Sauer. Dave shook his head. "I won't need that. You keep it handy." He dragged open the door on rain and cold and darkness. "Melvil may be right. Smithers may be back."

The tall iron gates with their chain draperies stood open. Spotlights from brown-and-gold County cars shone on them. The cars stood in the street outside the high, vine-grown walls, whose leafage sparkled and dripped. More cars were at the far end of the drive, by the tall, jigsaw-work porch. They were hidden by the overgrown shrubs and untrimmed trees, but lights said they were there. Dave left the Jaguar, crossed the street, showed a Japanese deputy his ID, and started to explain his presence.

The deputy said, "Lieutenant Salazar is expecting you."

He sat in his patrol car and used a dashboard microphone. His thumb came away from the microphone switch. A loud-speaker crackled, staticky, in the car. Dave couldn't make out the words, but the deputy told the microphone, "Ten-four," and hung it up. He leaned out of the car into the rain and called to another deputy in rain gear beside the gate, "Let this man through."

Men moved around the grounds with flashlights. Sometimes the light streaked a yellow slicker. Voices called through the darkness. Someplace off in the night, a siren wailed. The elegant etched glass of the front double doors was smashed out. Both doors stood open. Salazar waited in the doorway. Dave climbed the high, gaunt porch steps to him. Salazar looked disgusted.

"He got away again," he said.

"Is Gifford all right?" Dave said.

Salazar snorted and turned aside. "He tried to shoot that .30-30 of his. The rifle? It blew up. I don't think it had been cleaned in twenty years. Wonder is"—Salazar followed the beam of a flashlight toward the staircase—"it fired at all. Blew half his head off."

"Dear God," Dave said.

"He was trying to save lover boy." Salazar located a staircase on the second floor and went up it, Dave following. "And maybe he did."

"What about The Edge? Your people get here in time?"

"We can't hold them for much." Salazar moved along a hallway to a door that stood open on stairs leading to the attic. "Breaking and entering." Salazar climbed the stairs. "Carrying concealed weapons. Killing the dogs."

"Beautiful animals." Dave climbed after Salazar. "Not savage enough. Not against *Homo sapiens*." They reached the attic. Dave stopped to catch his breath. He ought to quit smoking. He asked Salazar, "How did you get here before me?"

"I live about ten miles closer." Salazar shone his light over the heaped trunks, cartons, packing cases. "I left word at the

160

substation out here to phone me at home if anything went down around the Gifford place. You said maybe Silencio was still here. I kept thinking about that. Look at this mess! You could hide King Kong up here." Shaking his head, he moved down the crooked, narrow aisle between the walls of dusty junk that were De Witt Gifford's legacy to an uncaring world. Dave followed. Salazar stopped. "Coroner hasn't come yet," he said.

The old man, what was left of him, still sat in the motor wheelchair. Salazar brushed him for only a second with the flashlight's glare and swung it away. Blood had spattered the portrait of naked Ramon Novarro, forever young, on the wall above the bed. Were he and Gifford together now? Dave didn't believe it, but he figured Gifford would have appreciated the thought.

Shoes clumped on the stairs below. Voices spoke. Someone laughed. The doorway at the end of the aisle of junk glowed with moving lights. Men's silhouettes filled the door. Someone called, "Body up here?"

"Over this way." Salazar shone his light along the aisle again, then backed to make way for the men to pass. They were big men, young. One of them carried a collapsed gurney, whose metal fittings clinked. To get himself out of their way, Dave stepped past the grisly old man and found himself in the tower room, where the tall, curved window panes were murky yellow from the lights of the patrol cars far below. Like a big dead white bird, the ledger lay open on the coffee table.

Dave pulled the reading glasses from his jacket pocket, also the penlight. He sat on the crackly old Empire couch and bent above the book, moving the thin beam of the penlight along the lines of Gifford's fussy, old-maidish writing, checking dates and times. He frowned and turned back a page. And almost spoke aloud. Gifford had lied to him about the Mercedes. He read the entry twice, closed the book, pushed glasses and penlight back into their pocket, and got up from the couch, smiling grimly.

In the attic, Salazar holding the light, the hulking youths had got the frail old body onto the gurney. They began steering it on wheels back along the aisle. Dave's foot encountered something soft, huddled on the floor. He bent for it and picked it up. Salazar shone his light on it. A woman's cerise velvet hat, turban-style, a crumpled satin bow at the back. 1920? Sometime around there. Dave took three steps and dropped the hat over the stooped back of the coroner's man, onto Gifford's body under its cover.

"You're kidding," the coroner's man said.

"He wasn't," Dave said, and watched as the gurney was half wheeled, half hoisted down the aisle. Salazar's flashlight played on the stacked trunks, crates, barrels again. Dave frowned, turned back, took the flashlight from Salazar, and carefully probed the cobwebs with it. "Good God," he said, and put the light back into Salazar's hand.

"What did you see?"

"It's what I don't see. There was a World War II life raft up here. It's gone. Which suggests that the place you'll find Silencio Ruiz is downstream."

"The creek? Have you seen how that creek is running?"

"People raft it for fun all the time," Dave said. "Why wouldn't he try it to escape being killed?"

"It's only a different way to be killed," Salazar said. "We've had four drownings in this storm alone. Teenagers, grown men. People are crazy, Dave."

"I wonder what makes them that way," Dave said. "Can you run a check on a license number for me, please?"

"A forty-year-old life raft?" Salazar said. "Laying up here all that time? It would be rotten."

"Probably," Dave said. "I need this number."

"In the morning," Salazar said.

19

The rain stopped in the night. The early-morning sky was clear of clouds and very blue above the chilly spur canyon called Concho. The water of the creek still ran hard and deep beside the crooked road, but the dips in the blacktop no longer held overflow. In a few hours the stream would be a trickle, the rocks and sycamore trunks dry again.

He stopped the Jaguar at the place where trucks left the road at night. He got out and stood gazing along the ruts between the oak tree trunks to the place of rusty barrels and dead ferns. Except for the rush and rattle of the creek, the canyon was dead quiet. Birds sang on a morning after rain. Not here. A breeze pushed at his hair. The breeze brought the bad smell from the dump.

He turned away and, wincing against the brightness of the sky, looked up at the house hanging off the canyon wall high above. No sign of life. Maybe whoever lived there was asleep. He had come early so as to catch them before they left for the day. To work? From a house like that? In a setting like this? Why not? It had to be paid for. Everything had to be paid for.

He got back into the Jaguar and drove on, looking for a road up. But all he found were bridges where the creek bent and the road found better footing on the other side. The road petered out after a couple of miles, where the canyon narrowed and a waterfall came splashing down among rocks and ferns to start the creek. He drove back the way he had come. The street map book showed no road along the ridge of Concho canyon, but he explored for it because it had to be there. It took a quarter of an hour.

The road on the ridge was no more than a driveway, one car wide, the asphalt almost new. It ended where a six-foot-high cedar plank fence ended. Dave parked beside the fence and got out into silence. The noise of the creek far below hardly reached here. Quietly he shut the Jaguar's heavy door, and he walked quietly to where a double gate of cedar planks was closed and padlocked. He peered through the slot. A Winnebago camper stood alone in a two-car port. It looked brand-new, meant to go everywhere, never been anywhere. Maybe this was wilderness enough for it. Another gate opened farther along the fence. A leather thong hung down beside it. He pulled this and sleigh bells rang.

But no one came. "Hello!" he called. "Anybody home?" His voice echoed in the canyon hush. No other voice spoke. He waited. He jangled the bells again. He called again. Then he took out his wallet, slid a shiny pick from it, and gently worked the spring lock that was a round shine of brass in the rough cedar. The gate opened on a narrow deck on whose rails stood potted creepers and succulents. Some of the succulents bore very small, bright orange flowers. Below the deck, the roofs of the house made sharp angles. He swung the gate to close it behind him, and its lower edge scraped envelopes. There was a mail slot in the gate. He gathered up the envelopes and closed the gate.

A prefab black iron spiral staircase went down from the

deck. He took it. Even his soft shoes made it gong. If the inhabitants were asleep, maybe that would wake them. The deck down here was wider, and trees in wooden tubs stood in its corners. The wall of the house that faced it was panels of sliding glass—closed, curtains drawn. Dave stood regarding it, absently straightening the edges of the pack of envelopes in his hands. He wandered down the deck, looking for a door. It was a double door, when he found it. Locked. He didn't know this type of lock.

An elaborate system of cedar-plank staircases and decks surrounded the house. Someplace there might be an open window or a door with an easier lock. He went from level to level, downward, where the shadows of the tall trees made the morning chill again. The room he got into without trouble was functional, wooden-walled, at one end a workbench under a neatly ordered rack of tools, at the other end a bare desk, a home computer, a file cabinet. A row of windows looked out into trees, the canyon slope falling off steeply below. He looked down. The road beside the stream was visible from here, though the tops of the oaks obscured the dump. Had the raw-throated roar of the big diesels in the silence of the canyon night ever wakened the people who lived here? Were they the ones who had agitated for the fallen signboard? He guessed he wasn't going to find out. Not today.

The desk seemed the right place to leave the mail. He laid it there, turned away, turned back. He dug his reading glasses from his jacket, put them on, blinked at the name typed on the top envelope. *Mr. Lorin Shields.* He frowned. Didn't he know that name? He sorted through the other envelopes. *Mr & Mrs. Lorin Shields. Jennifer & Lorin Shields. Lorin Shields.* He let the envelopes fall to the desktop. Hell, yes. Lorin Shields was the senior vice-president he'd waited for the other morning at Tech-Rite, met for a moment as the man had hurried on long legs out of the executive parking lot. Tall, thin, intense.

But Tech-Rite was thirty, forty miles from here. He stared at the envelopes. And inside his head, Shields's sleek oriental secretary said again, *He's rarely late. It must be the rain. He has a long way to come.* What had been the apple-cheeked lad's name out there? Jochim. The one so flummoxed by the picket line at Foothill Springs. He'd said something about Shields's wife. *He built her a glorious new house.* Dave saw in his mind's eye Shields's face again, under the dripping brim of an Irish tweed hat—drawn, tormented, pain in his eyes. And something else. Startlement, maybe even fear, when Jochim told him Dave's name. Dave had wondered then if he'd imagined it. What kind of sense did it make?

He climbed glossy inner staircases past stretches of polished plank flooring scarcely broken by isolated arrangements of furniture—never more than three or four pieces. He was reminded of those big, unused rooms at old De Witt Gifford's. Except that life had left those. Here, it looked as if life hadn't really had time to get started. The beautiful tall shafts reaching for light, the high sheets of glass framing the trees, the floating lofts and quiet wooden bays of the empty house didn't breathe or speak of a past or a future. Nor even of a present. In a bedroom that gave the effect of resting lightly in the tops of trees, only half of the wide bed had been slept in, sheets and blankets thrown back, one pillow dented. A lonely sight. In the house entryway, Dave took down from one of a row of thick wooden pegs an Irish tweed hat.

Somewhere a telephone rang, the jangle echoing in hollow, wooden vacancy. He stood holding the hat, listening, counting the rings. Did they mean that someone was commonly here at—he checked his watch—eight-thirty in the

166

morning? If so, would whoever that was return soon? It wouldn't be Shields, would it? This was a workday. To reach Tech-Rite from here and keep business hours, he'd have left long ago. His wife? The Jennifer of the envelopes? No. *Lost his wife recently*, Jochim had said. *Very suddenly. It was a shock. She was young.* Dave hung the hat back on its peg. The telephone stopped on the tenth ring.

Down in the workroom again, he pulled open the top drawer of the file cabinet. Like the desk, the cabinet was handsome dark Danish teak. But like the house around it, it hadn't had much use. The few manila folders in the drawer did not stand up. They lay on their backs in a loose stack, as if hastily dropped in and forgotten. He put the reading glasses on again, lifted the files out. TECH-RITE. *Shipping Dept. Do not remove.*

He sat down at the desk and leafed over the papers, yellow flimsy carbon copies of waybills. Two bore Paul Myers's signature. Dave couldn't puzzle out, from the strings of numbers and letters typed on the waybills, what he had carried. He hadn't trucked for Tech-Rite on the ninth, when he was killed. But one date did interest Dave. It was the date on the latest of the waybills in these folders—and it was the date on which the news broke that Myers's truck had not simply crashed but had been bombed. That was when Lorin Shields had brought these files home.

Dave took off the reading glasses and gazed down the room at the workbench. He folded the bows of the reading glasses, pushed them into their pocket, rose, dropped the files back into their drawer, rolled the drawer shut. He walked down the long room and crouched to look under the workbench. There hadn't been time for junk to accumulate there, not much, a few small empty cartons. And a shoe box—not empty. He lifted it, set it on the bench, took off its lid. Inside was a snarl of thin wires of many colors, switches, gadgets he couldn't name. But under these, each trim flat oblong wrapped separately in cellophane, was something he could name—soft, corpse-gray, and sticky. Plastique.

"Stand very still," a voice said. A man stood in the doorway to stairs that led up to the kitchen. Lorin Shields. Tall, thin. And bald. Checked sports shirt open at the throat, hopsack trousers, corduroy jacket, crepe-soled shoes. A revolver in his hand. Forty-five. The sort that U.S. law enforcement believes stops a man best. "Brandstetter," Shields said. "I suppose I knew it would be. I've read about you in the magazines."

"They exaggerate," Dave said. "They get things wrong."

"One thing they didn't get wrong," Shields said. "You never quit."

"If you'd kept out of it," Dave said, "I'd never have connected you."

"I was sure someone knew where Paul Myers had been that night. And why. This house is so near. I had to find them and stop their mouths."

"What had Myers done to you? Besides littering up your landscape?"

"Killed my wife," Shields said. "A lovely young girl. Do you know what she wanted from life? Everything gentle and beautiful. A house in the woods. Quiet. Solitude. Nature. Away from the world."

"You gave her that," Dave said.

"She went walking, didn't she?" Shields said bitterly.

"And stumbled on that dump," Dave said. "And died of uncontrollable diarrhea, coughing, paralysis of the diaphragm. The way Ossie Bishop died."

Shields's mouth spasmed at one corner. "Who knew who Smithers was? Not even you. He came to your house to kill you. Your wife saw him. Even after that, you didn't know. Who told you?"

"A sick old man you never even heard of," Dave said. "Crippled. In a wheelchair. You worried about the wrong thing, Shields. Do you know how H. L. Mencken defined *conscience*? 'The still, small voice that tells us someone is watching.'"

"Not now," Shields said. "No one is watching now."

Dave said, "But your conscience hasn't worked for a long while, has it? Your man Jochim told me that factory out there, Tech-Rite, meant everything to you." Dave looked around at the handsome room, the lovely setting outside the long row of windows. "It paid you well, didn't it? Bought you everything a man could wish for. Beautiful house, expensive cars, lovely wife. It didn't matter to you that it was poisoning people. Not till it poisoned her."

"We're going to take a walk," Shields said.

"And then," Dave said, "you didn't have the guts to plant your bomb at Tech-Rite, did you? Instead, you blew up some man whose name you didn't even know. You didn't know Myers. Wait a minute, maybe you did. You brought those cargo manifests home to hide them."

"I knew we were using gypsy truckers to get rid of certain chemical wastes we weren't authorized to dump at Foothill Springs. You don't understand how impossible all those government regulations make doing business."

"And the horrible thought suddenly struck you that maybe Myers had brought his load that night from Tech-Rite, so you snatched the papers. But you were mistaken. He didn't dump waste from Tech-Rite in your front yard."

"Not that night—no. But earlier someone had, Myers or Bishop or someone. I recognized the barrels. Our codes stenciled on the lids." He gave his head an impatient shake.

"It wasn't Myers. It was what he was doing. It was what he and his kind had done to Jennifer." His eyes were wet. He blinked them hard. He jerked the gun barrel. "Come on." He stepped up backward into the doorway. "And be very careful."

"A walk?" Dave said. "Where? Down to the dump?"

"It kills everything that touches it," Shields said.

He began climbing the narrow steps backward, the gun leveled at Dave's head. After the brightness of the workroom, the stairway seemed dark. Dave watched his step. It wouldn't do to stumble. A noise from the kitchen above made him raise his head. He knew that noise. He had made it often lately. It was the rasp of the slide, backward, forward, on the Sig Sauer automatic, the move made to get a bullet from the clip into the chamber.

Cecil stood at the top of the stairs in sunlight, gripping the gun in rigidly outstretched hands. His eyes were wide. His skin looked dusty. Shields heard the noise when Dave heard it. Shields tried to turn. Too quickly. He lost his footing. His gun went off. The Sig Sauer went off. The bullet thudded into Shields's chest and tore out through his back. Shields's blood spattered Dave's face. He tasted the salt of Shields's blood. Shields fell backward on him, and his dead weight was too much to hold up. Dave folded under it. He ended on his back on the workroom floor, struggling to free his legs. He wanted to get to Cecil. Because, up in the kitchen, Cecil was crying. It was the saddest sound Dave had ever heard.

Romano's was quiet in its candlelight. The white tables with their shimmering glassware and silver had been vacated long ago. Shadowy figures drank in the little bar where Max polished glasses. At the corner table, Dave sat back, smoking a cigarette, holding brandy in a snifter, turning it gently, watching Cecil. Cecil was telling Amanda how it had come to happen. He had already told the story several times today. Dave was hoping that telling it enough would free him of guilt and grief. He doubted, but he hoped.

"So then Lieutenant Salazar phoned. He had the information on this license number Dave had asked him for. From De Witt Gifford's record book. Smithers's Mercedes, right? And I wrote it down. It was at the desk, you know, in the back building. Those little Bishops hopping around."

"I love them," Amanda said, "but they do hop a lot."

Dave looked at his watch. "They should be sound asleep at the Hutchings house in Halcon by now. And Melvil too. I don't think he's had much sleep lately."

"That Duchess made a good substitute for nightmares," Cecil said. "So Melvil heard me say the address, as I was writing it down. And when I hung up, he came and read what I'd written on the pad. Concho Canyon. And he said Concho Canyon was where he took Dave. To show him the dump. Off Torcido Canyon. Where Dave went this morning. To talk to whoever it was that lived up there in that house."

"Shields," Amanda said, "who called himself Smithers."

"Turns out it was his wife's maiden name," Dave said. "Salazar was right. Who would hide behind an alias like Smithers?"

"So I tried to call Salazar back," Cecil said, "tell him to get up there right away. Only by then he'd already left the office. On his way to the beach. The LAPD found Silencio Ruiz's body. It washed clear down to the ocean. But I didn't learn that till later. All I knew now was that Dave was walking into Shields and he wouldn't be ready."

"I thought I was going to talk to people who might be able to tell me something about the dumping up there that

I didn't know. Something that might help me get to the Duchess. They had a marvelous vantage point, perched up there on the side of the canyon."

"Salazar had given me Shields's phone number too," Cecil said, "and I tried that. Don't know what I thought. What good was that going to do?"

"It would have done a lot of good," Dave said, "but I couldn't answer it, could I?"

"You didn't," Cecil said. He told Amanda, "Didn't leave me any options, did it? He didn't even have the gun. Left the gun with me, in case Smithers came around."

"He liked shooting in the early morning," Dave said. "Remember? He was shooting Louella Bishop while I waited for him at Tech-Rite."

"So I drove up there," Cecil said. "And, oh-oh, the Mercedes was there. And it was quiet. So quiet." He gazed at Dave across the candle flame, eyes round and ready to weep again. "And I thought, 'He's dead. Shields shot him.' But this time I had the sense not to make any noise. Last time—remember?—I went up to the door of that cabin and told everybody inside I was there, and they shot me full of holes. Not this time."

"And a good thing, too," Amanda said mildly.

"I climbed the fence. And tried a bathroom window. That's the one everybody forgets to lock. And inside the house, I heard them talking. And." He set down his brandy globe, pushed back the black velvet barrel chair, stood. "Can we go home now, please?" he said to Dave.

"Poor child," Amanda said. "You must be exhausted."

"I'm going back to television news," Cecil said. "There, whatever happens, it happens to somebody else."